Venable Park

VENABLE PARK

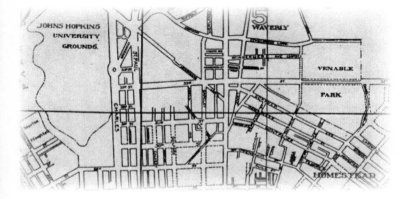

TOM FLYNN

Mill City Press
Minneapolis, MN

To Michael Augustus Flynn & Charles F. Zimmer
Soldiers of the Great War

Mill City Press, Inc.
212 3rd Avenue North, Suite 290
Minneapolis, MN 55401
612.455.2294
www.millcitypublishing.com

ISBN - 978-1-936400-29-4
ISBN - 1-936400-29-4
LCCN - 2010933827

Cover Design & Typeset by Sophie Chi

Cover image c. 1924 Baltimore Municipal Journal
Map image courtesy of Albin O. Kuhn Library, University of Maryland-Baltimore
County

Printed in the United States of America

PROLOGUE

On December 3, 1921, a football game was played on the campus of Johns Hopkins University in Baltimore pitting two unusual opponents against each other. The referees represented four different Ivy League schools, yet it wasn't a college game. It was instead a match between two military teams: the Army's Third Corps Area squad against a group of Quantico Marines.

The crowd overwhelmed tiny Homewood Field as civic hot air filled the skies above it. Anyone willing to listen was told that this game, in just its second year, stood only behind the venerated Army-Navy tilt as the most important military game of the season.

Quantico prevailed 22-0, dealing a setback to young Army assistant coach Dwight D. Eisenhower in the process. As Baltimore Mayor Joseph Broening looked on from his seat at midfield, he reveled in the crowd's enthusiasm for the game, and envisioned in the contest an opportunity to elevate his city's national stature.

In the weeks following the game, the mayor revived a civic notion adrift for a decade to build a major stadium in Baltimore and worked rapidly to make it a reality. It was proposed that the city's Mt. Royal Reservoir, no longer used for drinking water, be drained and a football stadium with baseball potential fitted within its sunken confines.

The revered former Baltimore Oriole manager Ned Hanlon lived in Mt. Royal, however, and sat on the Parks Board. He opposed the notion of 40,000 football fans in his neighborhood each fall weekend and proposed that the city's larger Lake Clifton be drained and fitted with a bowl.

En route to viewing Hanlon's suggestion, members of the Board spied nearby Venable Park, a park in name only. It was in truth an old brick quarry turned trash dump, rapidly filling with the used ash cinders that 1921 Baltimore spewed out at a prolific rate. Why not put the stadium there? The cinders weren't yet fully settled, and excavation could be done much more easily and quickly than at other locations.

With the president of the Parks Board, J. Cookman Boyd, now backing Venable, it was chosen, passing both Mt. Royal and Lake Clifton. Ground was broken in early May and a stadium of Olympian stature was promised.

What resulted instead was Venable Stadium, built cheaply and speedily in just seven months in 1922. A 40,000 seat horseshoe shaped bowl, it was erected substantially from dirt and wood with a modest concrete wall at its interior base (a classically-inspired façade would be added in 1923).

The required upkeep of the stadium in future years would become legendary.

On December 3, 1922, Venable Stadium opened to fanfare seldom seen in twentieth century Baltimore. Two members of the Cabinet and three governors were on hand, and a Marine sergeant called the play-by-play into a radio telephone linked directly to the White House. The Marines once again edged the Army, this time by a score of 13-12, and Baltimore was on its way to a future forged by toil, war, and ultimately, Venable.

CHAPTER 1

I live down at the Point in a boarding house. It's not the best place to live when the wind is up from the south and brings along the smoke from the stacks. If you look at it from the outside, the house is not much to see, with the soot so heavy on the white sills that you'd think they are gray. But when it's a land breeze and it takes the smoke back towards the water, then you have something.

The reason I live here, which is easy enough to figure, is I work at the mill. I don't work in the coke ovens or near the blast furnaces, so in that way my job is a little easier than some. On the other hand, when I am taking the trolley car north into the city and I watch the conductor sit and say, "Next stop, Dundalk," I think that trolley conductors might have a leg up on me and a few others at the mill.

This year I will take to writing some of my days down, as I have come upon something worth writing about, which is not the feeling that you have every day leaving a mill or if not particularly inclined to write. I will jump in here as the starting point because it is as good as any.

I am a company man, and I have done well by them, but I am trying to get ahead in this world. With buying from the company store, there is often little opportunity for that. The money comes right out to pay the store before you even see it, which can make you feel like you are working for hardly anything at all.

I work in a place that is hard to describe unless you are from Sparrows Point, and even then it would take a lot of particulars about the mill. I will assume for writing purposes that whoever reads this someday does not work at a mill.

My job is working in a small tower just next to the coke ovens. The smell from them comes up to us pretty regularly but thankfully not every day. The coal comes in off the railcars and then travels for a stretch on a belt to us. Once in the tower, gravity will take over and drop it into the coke ovens directly. After being baked in the ovens, just the coke is left to fire the blast furnaces, and the stuff you can't use is all burned off.

As the coal goes on a belt through my area some of it falls off and me and the fellows shovel it back on. That is a simple explanation of things, but it is complicated enough to give you the picture. When the coal falls off the belt, it hits and goes a lot of ways so you need to work steady with the fellow next to you as it is not easy to say that this piece that has fallen is yours or that piece is mine, especially with the noise from the belt and the nearby furnaces and ovens so loud you can't hardly hear. You have to work with somebody willing to more or less split things in half and who has a good eye for doing it.

So in that way, the fellows in my area are a little closer than in others, and if you get a bad pairing, it does not last long. We have had more than one argument up there, although with things so loud it is hard to say just when an argument is happening. Not all of our operation is indoors, but our part is, and we have a few windows in there that are pretty much covered over with dirt. The floor boards have been there forever and are good and solid and they're covered with dirt, too, so it almost looks like we are working on a dirt floor, but we are not.

To keep things straight, Beth Steel divided up stations on the belt by number, and I am station number five. Right before me is station number four, as you would guess, and working that station is a colored fellow named Reginald Spector. Some fellows around here are not partial to colored folks as a matter of course, but I more or less think about them based on what is happening at that particular moment, as I might anybody. And Reginald from moment to moment does a good job, especially if we get a big piece of coal that comes bouncing off the belt. He will just move on it and expect that I do the same back when the next one comes, and we do this pretty much without talking.

There is another fellow at station number six named Stanley Sowa who is good, too, but with Stanley about once a day I will have to point out somehow where his count is off and he should be doing more than he is. He is agreeable enough and usually changes how he's acting, but maybe he is not so good at adding or keeping track because the next day we are off the mark again, and more or less I say the same thing.

Well, a little about Reginald, he is 29 and two years older than me and living in a dormitory across the Humphrey's Creek clearing. We have figured out a pretty good system and have never given the foreman much reason to yell at either one of us. The negroes and the whites don't eat together in other parts of the mill, but where we work we often just sit down for awhile right on the spot when the belt goes off for twenty minutes around lunch. With only twenty minutes and us up in a tower, there isn't much reason to leave the room unless you are heading to the bathroom. Stanley usually sits down on the spot, too, but when things aren't going well some days on the work side you are not inclined to starting talking about old times at lunch, so we only talk about half the time.

I know that is pretty unremarkable, having three fellows having lunch at a steel mill in April, but one day Reginald mentioned that up in the city they were putting some new seats in Venable Stadium for the Army-Navy game late this fall.

His father works up there and from what Reginald says does pretty well for himself even though he's old. Venable was built mostly out of dirt and wood a couple years back in 1922. After a good rain the dirt is always washing down the sides, and the wood after just a couple years is already rotten and splintery in spots and needs to be replaced. At least that's how the *Sun* tells it. His father works the place like somebody might a farm, fixing and tending to things one right after another all day long.

One lunch he started in about his father.

"My dad's working round the clock to get ready for the game. Usually they got him just fixing things, you know, but he says to me that they're putting 40,000 new seats in, and he's doing lots more than that. They got some new boys helping out, but they don't know that place, my father says they do the work in twice the time it takes."

Reginald kept on, "So he asked me to come up there on Sundays when we're off here and help him out. So that would mean working every day regular."

That is a lot for sure, and Reginald just bit into this big piece of bread with butter and said something else, but his mouth was full, and it just came out as noise, so I sat and waited for him to figure out that all I heard was noise, but he didn't say anything else.

"What was that again, Reginald?"

He looked at me for a moment as if he was wondering about my hearing but the truth is for all the noise here my hearing is fine unless you're talking with a big piece of bread and butter in your mouth.

"I'm thinking about it."

I know Reginald pretty well now, and I know that lots of times he's telling you something without saying it, letting you figure out what he's really getting at. Maybe it comes from working the belt, leaving out parts of conversations to save time. Stanley does the same thing sometimes.

"You think they need somebody up there for shoveling coal back on a belt?" I asked, smiling a bit through the food.

Reginald ate some more and had to think, I guess, whether that was a joke, and it was, but it is not the best that I had ever told, and so he just kept eating and swallowed down some water from out of the outdoor fountain that he would fill up his drinking canister with each day.

"No, but they need fellows round the clock which tells me they just plain need fellows without too much care about the particulars. You can do something up there if you'd want. I can ask him."

This was good of Reginald to offer because even though we get along fine when the belt's running, when it's not we usually talk about nothing. So somewhere in that nothing he figured I might be interested in making some extra dough.

"Think they need a shovel?" I asked him.

"Henry, the way my dad tells me, that place is pretty much made of dirt, so I think if you know how to handle a shovel, they can use you. He's shoveling most times he's working just to keep the place from washing away. Yeah, I think they need some."

This sounded suitable to me, as they say.

"Well you go ahead and tell him I can work on Sundays. I don't know how many hours he's looking for, but I can put in a full day. On Sundays round here I don't do much other than get a bath and sometimes get to church. I can miss some church for awhile."

I go to St. Luke's on D Street on occasion, and to be honest, I often go just to put on a nice shirt and have a look inside a place that is better looking than the mill. I'm not generally fond of the inside of churches since my younger brother John was killed and we gathered for him at Holy Trinity back home. Still, Father McCabe keeps St. Luke's clean as a whistle despite the smoke and ashes. The belfry alone is one worth seeing. It's the highest spot in town that's not attached to a mill, and when the bells chime and you are heading up the steps looking at the stained glass, it's easy to forget the mill for a stretch.

Reginald nodded back at me. It was close to the end of lunch.

CHAPTER 2

My boarding house is on E Street, not too far from the clearing that once was Humphrey's Creek but now is all filled in. Reginald would head across the clearing to the north side, which was the colored section of town. We would walk back home together from the mill sometimes, along with Stanley, and after a day of work we might have something interesting to say about a machine breaking or the coal coming in heavy or it being hot or how the belt seemed to be moving a little faster or a little slower.

It was good enough talk, and it got us across town, and Stanley would turn up a block before me into one of the rowhouses on D Street, and that was that, and then I'd head off another block with Reginald. Sometimes it didn't go this way at all, and Reginald would fall in with a group of colored fellows, and me and Stanley would fall in with some of our boys. Stanley was married to a woman named Helen and she was nice enough, but didn't care for me much. She really disliked Reginald for being colored, but also because we were two bachelors and had no kids and slowed down Stanley's pace to what you might call very leisurely.

I can't blame her on the leisurely part, I must say, because Stanley has two kids and for some reason they are a just plain rotten pair. That is not something people should say all that often about somebody's kids, otherwise you come off as evil-spirited. I have to say it here, though, to explain why Helen could use having Stanley home and why that was understandable. She would sometimes have me over for dinner but not Reginald, and we never had to say anything to Reginald other than "bye," and he'd keep heading for the clearing, and we'd turn onto D. Tonight was one of those nights, but I threw in, "Let me know what your father thinks, Reginald."

He waved and walked on and Stanley and me started in towards his house.

Stanley's house was a brick rowhouse, just two in from the end of the street on the west side. They was always covered with soot so they looked a lot older than they was, but they were roomy enough, and solid, and a leg up on a boarding house. We were just a few feet from his front steps when damn if I didn't get hit with a rock thrown by one of his kids from the lower floor window. It caught me square in the cheek and stung like hell.

"Well Goddamn, Stanley, your kids can't even wait until I get in your house to be rotten!"

It came off worse than I wanted it to, but if you finish up a long hard day at the mill and are thinking about a nice dinner but instead get a rock in the cheek, that type thing might just fly out of you.

Stanley stopped in his tracks and stood there quiet, like he wasn't sure what to say, and then he told his son to close the window. Helen had the other front window open. She was preparing dinner and heard me let out with "goddamn" and "kids" and "rotten," which was all she needed—and she did not need much—to say, "Stanley, if that man thinks he can come up my walkway cursing at my children and then get a meal, he is sadly mistaken!"

She then slammed the window and skipped any mention of the rock that just hit me in the cheek. Their older boy, I should point out, is thirteen and it is not as if he just learned to throw or is a year or two past the diapers. He let rip good and hard and caught me square.

"I'm sorry, Stanley, but that hurt like the dickens. Your kids aren't always rotten. Just sometimes after they do certain things they seem rotten."

If you step back and look at what I said, saying somebody's kids aren't rotten, they just seem rotten, isn't really improving things.

"Sorry, Henry," said Stanley, "He's playing baseball now and he's always throwing things."

I wondered what baseball had to do with hitting a guy in the cheek with a rock, but I was looking to patch things up after cursing and having Helen slam the window on us, so I did not ask this. And it was *us* she was slamming it on, because Stanley would be in more trouble than me. I'd just head home and have some bread and butter and take a look at the cheek. He was the one heading inside and would have to explain his cursing friend who was often talking to a Negro when she saw him pass by.

"No, I'm sorry Stanley. A boy's a boy, and I cursed with the window open and Helen right there, which isn't much better than throwing rocks. I'll head off and I'll see you at the mill Monday. Tell Helen I'm sorry and tell the kid he's got good aim but, well, good aim at somebody's cheek, well..." I said it with a smile to show I wasn't smarting anymore and hoping maybe he'd finish the sentence for me to his kid. He just smiled and nodded, like we were back at the belt, and I walked home to my place on E.

The Point was laid out so you knew where you stood in life. I was just on this side of the clearing, which meant I was as close to the bottom as you could be on this end of the town. The houses from C Street on up were where the higher-up employees lived, and in between were people like Stanley that weren't real high up but had families and such or were somewhat high up and if things went well were supposed to move up the streets towards A. Guys like me got to know what it was like being in the better houses just by being able to see them. The folks in the better houses saw what was waiting for them if they started slipping over at the mill. Living on E marked me in town as not especially highly stationed.

Still, it suited me well enough. I will say the water could smell God awful on some nights. I do not know what exactly goes in it from the mill, but there are so many things you throw out when you're making steel that sometimes the steel seems like the smallest thing left. More than once there is smoke coming off the water near the mill, and judging by the color of water down at the bathing beach on some days, I'm happy not to know what exactly's going in there.

The boarding house was a nice place, and we had a bathroom on the second floor with a few bathtubs and a shower, which, given how much dirt we all brought in at the end of the day, was far more important than a fancy porch or fancy ironwork that you saw on the nicer places at the Point. I consider myself lucky that my room was up on the second as I could see out away from the mill. I was on the north end of the building and could sometimes open a window without having soot settling on the inside too quickly.

My room was not a lot to write about, but it did tuck in under one of the gables, so I had a better window along with the view. It was pretty quiet most of the time up there. After a hard day at the mill you could maybe wash off and lie down for a minute without some loud noise keeping you from it. This was not true of many places on Sparrows Point.

Bethlehem Steel assigned a full time caretaker to the house, and he lived on the first floor, so things were a little looser up on the second. His name was Fleming and he somehow ended up with the title of "porter" from the boys, and to his thinking it was one of some importance. He was a little bit fat and had reddish cheeks that sagged down on both sides, like they was heavier than his mouth. He had some hair left, not a lot, but the company gave him a hat that looked like a train car conductor's and he wore it regular so you usually did not notice the missing hair. Porter Fleming would give advice on all things under the sun, and with his job of keeping the single men out of trouble and the boarding house running, I will give him that he had some valuable words to offer. He is maybe 45 but a good bit wiser than his years, as the boys will age you in a hurry with some of their nonsense.

He has, in my time since arriving here, told me how to mend a broken fence the right way, salute a colonel in a way likely to lead to promotion (although I was the one coming out of the service), soft boil an egg, and write an adventure story that every child will want to read if I put it down just how he says to and don't use profanity.

"Evening, Henry. You been in a scrape again?" was Porter's greeting.

I held my hand up to my cheek, and sure enough, it was bleeding. I pressed on it to slow the bleeding and stood still for a minute.

"Of course, Porter, some communist came up to me and said Beth Steel's been exploiting me. So I lit into him."

This threw him off because if a communist had said that about Beth Steel, Porter might have mixed it up with him. He liked the idea of it but wasn't so sure I was telling it to him straight.

"You put a steak on that Henry and hold it still for ten minutes, and the swelling will go down, and you'll be set," he said, turning to his bag of advice, which was not small.

"If I come across a steak, Porter, it's not going against my cheek."

He laughed at that, and things were okay, and he was not a bad fellow. He liked me well enough because he heard the boys on the first floor more loudly, so in his opinion the second floor boys were a pretty good bunch.

That was that with Porter, and I walked up the stairs with my hand still pressed on my cheek until the bleeding stopped. Stanley's kid had really let rip and that rock just might have been a piece of coal the way it cut me.

I had my own little icebox in the room which wasn't always cold in the summer but still a place to stow your food sealed up from the bugs and most of the time I kept something in there. I had some sausage and buttered bread then set into the *Sun* for a good couple of hours to catch up on things in the world. With that done I drifted off to sleep.

I will tell you about my dream that night, because I have this type more than I will say and they leave me feeling nearly run through. In it there was a ridge, I do not know where. It was close at hand, and not high, maybe just the size of one fellow standing on top of another's shoulders. On the far side of it

was John. I couldn't see him but I knew he was there.
I looked into the night air for him and just as I did a
shell hit to my right and I was struck onto my back,
knocking my helmet from my head. I felt my shirt to
see if I was hit. I couldn't feel my shirt at all and just
kept trying, but there was nothing.

"Get back!" I yelled to John just before another
shell landed. This one was farther off, or it felt that
way with the ground shaking a little less. He rarely
took heed of me in Poughkeepsie and here we were
in the fight and he paid me no attention at all.

"Henry, you catch up with me or leave me be!"
I heard John call back. There was a shell screaming
towards me again and I dove and took cover. It
hit, and dirt and mud splattered on me and I was
covered up to my neck the next I knew. I couldn't
move and my chest was pressed so tightly with mud
I could hardly get enough air in.

"John, come back!" I yelled. It was dark and
smoke settled heavy down on the ground like you
might see right after the fireworks on the Fourth.
Hills sprung up around me now, and they came up
so quickly it felt like I was sinking. He was nowhere
that I could see and I still could not move. I could
turn my head enough to see a horse out in the open
just before the hills. It stayed still, unbothered by
all of this, and turned its head towards me when I
screamed John's name again. A final shell blew and
I covered my head and when I looked up the horse
was down on its side and bleeding, its head rocking
up and down off the ground and its legs kicking at

the same time. It whinnied horribly and I tried to get up but I could not, my arms pinned now and nothing able to move. The ground got colder around my chest and I pressed up like a shot to get free.

With this I woke up, my arms tangled in my bed sheets and my nightshirt soaked straight through. The dream is like the others, yet it is as terrible as the first. I turned on the little lamp next to the bed, picked back up the *Sun*, and worked through the pages like I was reading them for the first time. My hands was shaking so badly it took some time just to start in.

CHAPTER 3

Monday morning came and it was time to head back down to the mill again. It being April, the air was starting to warm up a bit when you woke up, and that made getting up easier. I usually fell in with pretty much anybody on the walk to work, as neither me nor Stanley nor Reginald would get to the same spot at the same time, and we were too old to try too hard to.

As it happens and lucky for me, Reginald was coming up across the clearing. I could see him from my window after I'd polished off my dried sausage and bread. I washed it down with some milk from the Sparrows Point Dairy. I have to say the milk is far better than what I got in the service, which was usually the lowest grade they make and I'm not sure entirely from a cow. The dairy was right near Penwood Park, and you could get it fresh most any day, which is more than they could say in some of the better places around the world.

I slicked my hair back to get it out of the way, pulled on my cap, and then headed down towards the front door.

"Morning, Porter," I said as I passed him by.

"Morning, Henry. The cheek's looking better. The steak worked then, did it?"

Where I'd turn up a steak I'd never know. "Yeah it worked. You oughta be in the fights, Porter."

He smiled, pretty pleased with his good advice. And then I was out the door. Reginald was coming up with a crowd of colored fellows, and I did not join him. I kept my distance and just fell in stride, and eventually the colored fellows split off to their places at the mill, and Reginald and I headed up to our spot at the belt. Once up in the tower, I could hear the echo of Stanley's steps coming up the metal stairs below.

"Morning, Stanley," was all I got out before the belt was on and we were out of the talking portion of the morning.

It was hotter than on Friday, and we'd get good and warm up there today.

I have laid out the general way our day went, and Mondays in particular were never much different. Once in awhile by Wednesday we'd have a backed up shipment of coal or by Saturday we'd be polishing off a week's supply, so we'd be in a hurry, but Mondays came and went the same way most every week of the year.

The foreman lit into Stanley a little in the morning, but about what, I am not sure. He is not overly particular in what he yells about, so it's tough to guess. He once gave me an earful for not going by Hank instead of Henry, saying Hank was a lot easier. I told him he could call me Hank all he wanted because I couldn't hear him with the belt on, anyways. This did not sit well with him, and so he made a point of yelling "Henry" at me after that. I'd heard many a sergeant louder than that foreman and wasn't too impressed by yelling.

At lunch we knocked off, and all three of us just took a seat down right where we were.

"I got up to see my folks yesterday," Reginald said.

"Your dad mention the jobs up there?" I asked.

"He did. He said he'd put in a good word and maybe they'd give you a day a week. Show up next Sunday morning. I got in a half-day yesterday, and it went off pretty well."

That felt funny for a minute, a colored fellow putting in a good word to get me a job and with Stanley behind me and listening.

"Will a good word from him help, Reginald?" I asked.

He sat for a moment, looked at Stanley and me, and had things squared away pretty quickly, I imagine.

"It'll help, Henry," he said.

"I'll be up there Sunday," I said, and we were done.

This week was unremarkable. The coal came in, and some stayed on, and some fell off the belt, without much that would jump out at you. They said that on some days during the war it was the busiest place on earth and there is more than one textbook written that will bear that fact out. They forged the steel here and built ships, and they came out quickly, and the coal was needed to fire everything up. Those weeks they tell stories about, but they will not mention this one.

By Saturday's whistle I'd put in a good week, as had everyone around me, and I walked on home, this time alone. I'm not sure why that was, but Stanley and Reginald must have been off to other things. That was fine with me as I walked home a little quicker than usual to think through things for the next morning.

There was not a lot to think through, but I did have to figure out whether I should dress nicer than normal to make an impression that would land me a job, or whether I should just wear my work clothes so I could start right away if I got it. What I settled on was in the middle, work clothes that I had just laundered and that happened to be the best I had. You bought everything from the company store down here, and they were not inclined to run a special on things that millworkers needed like work clothes. You could pick up yourself some nice clothes for church, though, at a real break because I think the mill wanted to nudge you in that direction.

With thoughts about what to wear settled in my head, I drifted off to sleep pretty easily that night.

* * *

The next morning gray skies had settled over the Point. Rain is no stranger down here in spring, but it'd been dry most of the month throughout, so I

22

noticed it this time. I took the 26 up over Bear Creek towards the city. It is a sketchy matter taking that trolley over the creek as it doesn't quite fit the tracks right and every lurch has you wondering if you're going in the drink, ass over tea kettle. I think it helps to be tired when crossing so you nod off through the shaking and don't heed it all that much. I met Reginald on the 26 early, and about a half hour later, after switching trains, we was on 33rd street pulling up towards Venable.

As I said, the stadium opened up just two years ago. Before that there was Venable Park, which was really a half-filled old quarry. I remember reading where a little boy drowned in there once, which tells you how much of a park it was. It was a good idea to put a stadium in there because we got some good football games and all sorts of events. It made Baltimore feel more like a place you'd come to and not just a place you worked in or lived in because it just happened that way. But because of how quickly it was built, it took a lot of work to just keep it on as a working stadium.

When I got back from the war, I spent some time staying on in the service back at Camp Upton on Long Island. Once I'd moved on to Baltimore and landed a spot with Beth Steel I took a place at the boarding house straight off as rents at the Point were a fair amount lower than they were in the city. I hadn't been up for a game at Venable yet, but I followed it in the papers pretty closely and had seen the photographs. The pictures did not do it justice.

The entrance was all fine plaster, painted white and fresh with columns on both sides and a pair of matching tunnels on either side for you to walk through to get to the field. Coming from the Point, which had St. Luke's but not much beyond that, it was about the grandest place I'd seen in the States. I'd pick up the paper and read about what they was doing out in Chicago with the stadium in Grant Park and all that, but certainly that was something I'd likely never see. This was right here and all in white like the finest statue, and now I was going to try to get a job working in it. It was hard to imagine.

While I was busy looking up at the front, Reginald got ahead of me.

"Over here, Henry," he called back to me as I sort of pulled out of daydreaming and came back to why we was there.

We walked over to the very center of the entrance, which had a building built into it. It had eight white columns that stretched up over two stories where they met at the roof to form sort of a porch, but the nicest you have ever seen. I cannot imagine the White House looking much nicer. I should have dressed up more.

"You go in there, tell them your name and that you're Harold Spector's apprentice."

"Apprentice, Reginald? What am I apprenticing at?" I asked him.

There was no mention of my being an apprentice on the ride in or at any other point since we'd been talking about this job. Reginald left some big holes in a conversation sometimes.

"Don't worry about that. You get yourself over to my dad, and you're set. My father's colored, but he works hard and they respect him around here, at least some do. You're his apprentice."

He turned then and walked away, as if that sewed it up neat as a pin and there wasn't another word to be said about it. Down at the Point no wasting words was a good idea, with the belt moving and all, but out here in front of these white columns, I could have used a little more material to get a job with. Reginald was no further help, now gone away to one of the big ramps that flanked the sides of the entrance and climbed up to the top of the stadium. It was just me.

I took a breath for a moment, trying not to think of the place as that grand. After all, it was just a football stadium that on its best days had a bunch of guys running into each other right in the middle. I took off my cap, brushed my hair back to the side, and walked through the front door.

There were people coming and going, and I had no idea which way to turn. Finally I saw a door to my right that had smoky glass like some of the managers rated down at the mill. It had a taped piece of paper on it that simply read "Work," and sure enough, that was what I was here for, so I opened it and walked a little ways in.

Inside it was pretty big, and the floor was made entirely of white tile like you might see in a fancy kitchen. At the far corner of the room was a man sitting behind a desk. He looked about fifty or so and bald with hardly a hair left. He was wearing those little round glasses that a doctor or professor might wear, and that did not make me feel at ease, coming from a mill like I was. He was also holding his chin up a bit like you saw the British officers do once in awhile. This did not help, either. British officers and professors weren't really the type of fellows I might have over to play a game of checkers.

"Yes, sir?"

Since he used "sir" with me, I thought it fitting that I use it back.

"Sir, I'm Harold Spector's apprentice."

He paused, pushed up his glasses, and looked me over for a moment.

"You're not colored."

I knew that. I was hoping it wasn't one of those tricky questions they get you with to see if you're fit for the job.

"I am not. You're correct, sir."

This was not the right response, I knew straight off, as his face looked red all of a sudden, and his head snapped up from looking at a paper in front of him.

"That supposed to be funny, son?"

He'd dropped the sir, and was talking different altogether.

"No, sir."

I left it at that because if telling somebody they was correct about something got them mad there wasn't any use saying more.

"The job is for coloreds."

I guess nobody had told Reginald's dad the job was for coloreds, since he is, and there wouldn't be much need for telling him that.

"Yes, sir."

He waited for me to say more I think, but I knew well enough when it wasn't going to help me, so I left it at that and let him have the next words.

"What's your name?"

"Henry Dawson, sir."

"Dawson, my name is Hadley Overman. You apprenticed before?"

Now my head was starting to swim a little. At the mill some of the better-paying jobs you'd apprentice for but shoveling coal on a belt, well, that wasn't one. You took the shovel, and if you did it well enough, nobody stopped to tell you that you was fired. I was in trouble right now, so I threw out something that was true.

"I got pretty handy with a lot of things in the war, and after that I worked at the mill, and I am pretty good at my job, sir."

He paused again.

"You in the war?"

"Yes, sir. 77th Division. 308th Infantry."

"The 308th? In the Argonne?"

He asked me as if he didn't believe it, maybe because many of the fellows who went in there from the 308th are dead now. I was relieved we weren't talking about apprenticing anymore and instead something that I was familiar with.

"Yes, sir."

But, I wasn't going to go on about it. For all I knew, he only liked certain boys coming out of the Argonne, and I wasn't going to be the wrong type now that we were getting past my not being colored.

He looked at me long and quiet. I don't know what he was thinking, but my guess was he was trying to figure out if I'd work hard or not.

"They ever toss you in the stockade?"

"Never once, sir."

"Ever get away with something they should have thrown you in the stockade for?"

I would not trip on that one.

"Never once, sir," I repeated.

"How are you with the shovel?" he asked.

"I use it every day at the mill and used it just about every day in the service. I haven't had a problem yet and have dug myself some fine holes," I said, a little proud.

He kept looking at me, staring. I was solid enough, and no big belly to slow down the shoveling. After a little while his eyebrows rose up just a little in a good sort of way, if that makes sense.

"Okay, then. Fill in this sheet and put it in the box there," he said, waving at a little box at the corner of his desk like it was in another room because his desk was so big. "Then go out the way you came in, turn left, and head to the far side of the entrance. Harold's over there, and you'll know who he is."

He said that as if it was a question, wondering I bet if I even knew what Mr. Spector looked like, which I didn't. I filled in the paper as fast as I ever wrote anything, even with my hand shaking, and I put it in the box.

"Thank you, sir."

With that I was out the door before he could get in another question, and turned left. Sweat was running down my forehead now like it was the middle of July.

CHAPTER 4

Sometimes something easy comes after something hard, and sure enough it turned out it was real easy finding Reginald's father. Both are about 6 feet tall I'd say and thin as a wire. They look damn near the same except his dad's hair was all gray and his face is a little pulled down from the years weighing on it. I walked up towards him, and he stood waiting for me. Reginald must have told him what I looked like.

"Henry," he said, more telling than asking, and holding his hand out to me.

"Yes sir."

"You get the job?"

"Well, I got directions to where you are, and here you are, so I think I might."

"You tell them you was my apprentice?" he asked.

"That's what I told them."

"They think that was funny or peculiar?"

"He was expecting me to be colored, and I wasn't, so that was peculiar for him, I suppose. It wasn't for me."

I looked around because it sounded funny, and after all that business inside, I was looking for a laugh, so I let out a good one. Mr. Spector couldn't help it either, so only a minute into things and we were laughing hard. I figured that was a good start. But a white man and a Negro laughing hard together at a job during working hours is a swell way to get fired, so we covered up pretty quickly.

After the laughing I was out of words, having said more so far today than I might after two days at the Point. Fortunately Mr. Spector was not the stand-around type. Without another word he handed me a shovel, and we got to walking up the ramp on that side. It was mighty high and took you clear up to the top of the stadium.

What was waiting for me at the top, I will have trouble describing, given my limitations, but I will try. Down to my left at the bottom of the hill was the greenest field I'd ever seen. It was all mowed in lines, and there wasn't a speck of dirt down the middle. I do believe it had just been cut and the grass was almost shining. Around it was a cinder track for races like I imagine you might see in the Olympic Games.

If that wasn't enough, circling the outside of the track there was more of the greenest grass, and circling that a concrete wall about five feet high that was done up like it was stone or marble. Hell, maybe it wasn't concrete at all. It had little rectangular designs in it and the wall was like a frame around everything. You have to understand that at the mill the only things they built was for working, and you just didn't see anything like this. I am not the type fellow to say this, but it was beautiful. I almost fell forward down the hill just looking at it all.

Reginald's dad saw me, and since it was still just me and him, he didn't hustle me on immediately like he might have had to if somebody was watching.

"Like the front lawn of Paris out there. Worth all this work," he said, stepping up next to me to look longer at something he must have seen every day.

"Hard to imagine," was all I could come out with.

We had our moment looking at it, and then it was time to turn back the other way. The grass was green as clover, but the slope that ran out from the stadium was altogether different. First off, it clearly had done some settling since it was built because there was spots that just sank like something heavy pressed on them, but nothing had. Down at the bottom of the slope, was a little house that in its way was as nice as the front gate, only small and not as grand. Turns out that it was a ticket booth, of all things, and now I could add a ticket booth to the list of nicest things I'd seen in the last hour. Our job for today was working the slope.

"If we just let it be, this whole hill would be down on top of that booth," Mr. Spector said, pushing his hands forward to give the picture of it going down. "We need to work on this slope, keep the grass steady, and hope that someday it's just a hill without much help. Right now it's a pile of dirt, and it wants to get back down to where it came from."

With that, we started our way down the hill and stopped at the different places where there was something wrong with it—no grass, a gully opening up, rocks poking out from the ground, that sort of thing. For each problem, Mr. Spector told me more or less how to fix it on the spot, but he did so like he was talking to himself, awfully fast and awfully quiet and explaining like I knew it already.

"This here...like that," he'd say, and before I knew it, a little gully that had opened up would be filled with dirt, and then he'd pat down the end and say, "and make it tight."

Then we'd be onto some missing grass or some gravelly dirt—"Half this hill ain't dirt, it's ashes"—and then he'd point to a dark patch or another and we'd have that squared away.

So it went for the morning, and we made a lot of trips up the hill to get fill dirt. There was so much wrong with this particular part of the slope that we never got too far, only moving back and forth to the problem spots and then up the hill to get some fill or back down the hill to pick up something. My legs were aching from working on the slope, but Mr. Spector seemed not to mind it even though he was no spring chicken. He had a system, though, and was good at keeping the trips up the hill to as few as possible, picking up things that fixed problems we hadn't even gotten to yet, sort of like he was reading a map I didn't have. It was hard work, and lunch time felt like dinner, and the final whistle like it was time for bed.

Since it was Sunday, we was done by 4:00. It was not a hot day, breezy at times even, but with all the work, my face was covered with dirt, and I was sweating like it was a hundred out.

Mr. Spector set down his tools, then took out a rag, wiped off his face, and half-smiled. He had some water for the both of us, and this was particularly handy as my canister was perfectly full and sitting on my nightstand at the boarding house.

"You did alright Henry. You handle this next Sunday?"

I didn't know exactly what he meant by "this." It sort of sounded like he was leaving and I'd be on my own.

"I can handle it, Mr. Spector. You're not leaving are you?"

He paused for a moment, wiped his face again, looked at the rag which was already grimy before he used it, and seemed surprised by the dirt. He then looked back at me and smiled.

"Not leaving but I'm not living or working till a hundred, neither."

He made it sound like that summed up things, which it didn't.

"Okay, Henry, I'll stay up here and check in with a few boys and then get things in place for tomorrow. You go ahead down and say goodnight to Reginald for me."

He then offered me his hand, and I shook it. It felt as gravelly as the ground.

CHAPTER 5

There is not a lot to tell about the ride home that day or the time after that or the next. Porter Fleming saw me come home Sunday nights covered with dirt.

"Save some energy for the mill, Henry. They butter your bread no matter what else comes."

This was just like Porter, as it took Beth Steel's general view of the world, included some advice, and worked in a saying like butter your bread just in case a dope like me couldn't figure out what he was saying in plain English.

There were good parts and bad parts about starting up in April, most all of it having to do with the weather. One Sunday it rained and there was no work, but not having a phone and not wanting to put Porter onto just what I was doing exactly, I didn't call anyone to figure out if work was on from the house phone. Reginald couldn't get at a phone at all, so we both got on the trolley up to the city and spent a good long while going into Baltimore in the rain for nothing. Another Sunday the slope was wet from the day before, and all I did that day was slip and fall and chew up more of the ground than I was fixing. It was aggravating, especially since it was overcast with no wind and the stadium stayed wet all day. But there was one Sunday at the end of April when the weather was perfect, a nice little breeze clearing out the sky and us working under the sun and enjoying it in a way I have never enjoyed a day at the mill.

On those Sundays it was still hard work, but it was part of something special, and you felt like you was adding to the city. After a month I took to thinking, just a little, like the stadium was an important thing that I was really helping along. That hill certainly would have been worse off if I wasn't working it, that wet Sunday aside, and I could picture in my mind that out in late November, 80,000 people were going to come in here and fill these seats and for one afternoon make this one of the top places in the world.

Now the mill in April was not a bad place either. We was inside on a rainy day, and especially on the cold days early on it was awful nice to work at a job that warmed you up a bit. I knew come July that would be the last thing I wanted, but you have to, in this particular case, take the view that you will leave that until July. But coming into the mill was not like coming past the Administration Building in front of Venable. No columns, no decorations, just everything there because it needed to be, or not there at all. And working with the belt, all the work did was bring more. You never got the feeling of getting ahead, just that you wasn't falling behind. It was different at the stadium.

It took a month, and another trip down to see Hadley Overman, to get things straightened before I got a paycheck for the Sunday work I was doing.

He remembered me sure enough because he said to me, like we'd just stopped talking,

"The Argonne did you say?"

"Yes, sir."

He then looked at me again, maybe trying to figure if I was just saying that. I heard about boys coming back and bragging about things they weren't part of, but that's not the usual thing. You just read a lot about it when it happens and they do a little checking, and it turns out the fellow was working in a shoe store when he said he was in the Argonne. None of us wanted to be there, and coming out, few of us talked about it much. Major Whittlesey felt the worst about things in the end. He was our leader in the Pocket, as they called it, and the weight of the men lost there was more than he could bear. One night after the war he stepped off the side of a steamer that was heading to Havana. They say he got up from dinner that night without a word about his intentions and went ahead through with it. It weighed on him that heavy.

After looking me over, Overman had me fill out a couple short forms, then took his pen and pointed towards the box at the corner of his desk.

"Check your mail, Dawson, and it will be there soon enough."

He was good on his word, and within a week a check arrived. Since Porter put our mail in the slots, he knew when anyone got something. He felt especially important if somebody got a big package, which he would always say had been entrusted to him. He'd say something like "Henry, a very large package with your name on it has been entrusted to me," as if it was an official ceremony that took place when the postman dropped it off and it was only because of Porter's place in polite society that the postman hadn't heaved it out the window.

I never got a very large package, but that's what he would've said. Porter was this way with official documents, too, and my first paycheck must have looked very official being as it was stamped with the return address "Baltimore Administration."

"Something from the mayor, Henry?" he asked, handing me the letter.

"Yes sir, Porter. I think he wants to come and speak to us fellows about whether we're getting a fair shake down here. It's so fair, Porter, I'll tell him he needn't bother to ask."

He did one of those half-smiles that people put on when they don't know if they're being poked fun at but had better smile a little anyway so they show they got the joke.

"Well, better not keep the mayor waiting. I'd hold it up to the light before I opened it because if it is official, it might just run up to the edge."

I waved it at him, saluted, and ran up the stairs. I got to my room and held it to the light and ripped carefully.

There it was—a yellow and white check from the city of Baltimore and written to me. I've got a birth certificate somewhere and my discharge papers somewhere else, but this was the best looking document with my name on it I'd seen in awhile.

* * *

Now there's a funny thing about the mill. They're strict and all, but there's certain things they don't mind you doing, so they make them a little easier to happen. One thing was getting to the bank. The bank was in Sparrows Point—pretty much everything you needed was somewhere on the Point—on the corner of 5th and D Street. It stayed open a little late on Friday nights, so people could cash their checks, but they also would keep it open a little late on Mondays, so if you still had money by the end of the weekend, you was maybe likely to put it in then.

It was nothing fancy, the Bank of Sparrows Point, and it was in a nice little square stone building with bars over the windows and some ivy growing up it. I went down there that day after work, which happened to be a Friday, to deposit my check.

The company wasn't crazy about you moonlighting so I kept it kind of quiet. Part of doing that was to pick out a teller at the bank who wouldn't make a big fuss about my check from the city. I walked over to Mrs. Foss after a long wait on the line.

Her old man was in the war and didn't make it back, so we talked a little bit more than usual whenever I made a deposit but she was always professional. She'd sometimes ask me something about France and I would help her out with what I knew. It was something in common even if we'd both wished it wasn't. She worked behind one of those little caged windows that let you slip the money under but not jump over the top to help yourself to the safe.

"Hello, Henry!" she shouted at me.

I was in trouble out of the gate. I forgot Mrs. Foss was hard of hearing, and that sometimes crossed over into her talking. When it did she shouted pretty loud, whether or not it was something worth shouting about. I don't know why I didn't figure on that.

"Here you go, Mrs. Foss."

I slid the check under the window, and she took a look at it, along with the deposit slip I'd put with it.

"You quit here, Henry?" she shouted.

With it being a Friday, the place was filled up, and many a head turned towards me to figure out who had done the quitting.

"No, I haven't, Mrs. Foss," I said as quietly as I could, looking down at the floor.

She looked at me, saw me looking uncomfortable, and got a little quieter. Even though she was about my age, when she tried to whisper it came out all raspy and hoarse like she was 100. I know she was doing her best, but it was a little alarming hearing it coming from a pretty woman, which she was.

"Okay, Henry," she whispered, and this was still pretty loud but surely quieter than her regular voice. She then did it one better to get things straight and said, "The usual?"

"Yes, the usual."

The usual, in my case, was putting it all in and leaving me $1.50 to get by with.

This check was for $12.37, so I put a nice-sized amount in before coming away with around-town money.

CHAPTER 6

Coming home from the war in May 1919 my folks greeted me at the docks right there by South Street in New York. There was a big throng of people and I really had no way of knowing if they would be there at all. My mother worked in a house for a wealthy family in Poughkeepsie on weekends and here it was a Saturday, so I did not expect her. She learned some proper English while working which she always tried to pass along to me. You can see it has found little purchase. My father was a bricklayer, and did not struggle for jobs but never got past being a bricklayer, either, and he was getting on fifty years.

Coming down the gangplank I spotted them straight away, which was about as lucky as could be considering the crowd and all. My mother hugged me hard, crying the whole time like a mother will. Word had made it to me that John was dead, and I'd written home to tell them as soon as I knew. They'd got word already, and that was back in January. My mom wrote me a little note back saying they'd heard, but I hadn't got another letter after that and here we was in May. It made a guy feel pretty bad, his younger brother killed and him coming back without hardly a scratch.

My father shook my hand and said, "Henry." He was all red in the eyes and kept looking past me back up the gangplank. He might have been drinking or crying, knowing him as I do it was likely both. He was a good man but Murphy's had him squarely in its grip and would not let go.

We took a train that day back up to Poughkeepsie without hardly a word. We live a block down from Holy Trinity and there was six boys from town lost in the war from the parish. I was on one of the last ships home and there was a handful of us from town, so they had a memorial service for all six boys just the next week. If you can picture a funeral, picture one for six and you will see that this was not a good idea for easing anybody's pain. My mother sat in the kitchen the morning of the service like she was struck ill. The rain was coming down in buckets outside and there was thunder and lightning every little while, shaking the window frames like a baby's rattle. I had on my uniform and hat, which set her off into tears as soon as she saw me. My father came downstairs right after me. He'd already been at the Murphy's and made no show of it being otherwise.

"How many boys over there and we lose ours?" he shouted, the smell of liquor filling our tiny kitchen. He did not look at me.

"Get her along to the church by 10," he shouted again and walked back out of the room. I felt the front door slam. The house shuddered with it, worse than from the thunder. My mom went further into tears and would not stop. It had been like this every day since I was home. I made up my mind right then to try to latch back on at Camp Upton.

* * *

The company was good to us and I have no complaints, but it was, like I said, hard to get too far ahead with the money you spent at the company store and all. There wasn't a lot of spare time to spend it, so the lack of money didn't hit you too hard, but there was still hardly a scrap to put away if it was grocery week or you needed some new shoes or what have you. With me working up at Venable all through the spring I was making a little extra and also was now working seven days a week, which made it easy not to spend. An exciting evening for me meant a good night's sleep. And so for the first time, the money slowly began to add up.

By June life was improving, truth be told. Mr. Spector taught me how to work the grounds of Venable and often times he would go off to show the newer boys how to do different things and wouldn't come back for a few hours. My job still was mainly working the slopes coming off the stadium, which it is no exaggeration to say were more than enough to keep one man busy.

When things were in pretty good shape there they would also let me dig some ditches, because they was running new wiring into the stadium and somebody got the idea to put it underground so the whole place didn't look like a bird's nest with all the wires wrapped around it. That was pretty clever.

Generally speaking, the stadium was coming along well. Mr. Spector would sometimes point out to me the wavy nature of some of the new seats they put in for the game. This was not surprising since the new seats were propped up by trusses that went into the ground, and they were still shifting. I would be awfully surprised if they held up for much longer than the football game this fall, but the game was about as far as they had in mind when they was adding on to Venable.

Mr. Spector didn't complain to anybody about the seats because that would have gotten him in trouble and the seats not fixed. He knew what he had a say in and what he didn't.

CHAPTER 7

Come summer I hadn't taken a day off since April, and it was beginning to wear me a little thin. I knew I couldn't work at the stadium forever, but I wasn't sure when I would stop. They seemed to need me every minute I was there. There weren't any real lulls during the day other than squeezing in a short lunch.

We don't hardly get any holidays during the year at the mill, but we do get the Fourth of July, and I was looking forward to that. The Fourth came up on a Friday this year, which was as good as any because I'd be working the next day no matter what.

I was fixing to have myself a little fun on my first day off in months. Down toward North Point but pretty close to Sparrows was a place you may have heard of called Bay Shore Park. It has been around a long time and is my favorite spot even though I can only get out to see it maybe once a year if things fall into place.

If you don't know, it's an amusement park right on the water, and if it isn't the nicest place around, I am not sure what is. It is easy to get to by the trolley, and I think it was even built by the trolley line to give people a reason to make the trip. To make it even better, the car will take you right there and roll you in under the rollercoaster, which by itself is exciting.

Thursday night I stayed up a little late, trying to make something out of the evening and then planning on visiting the park the next day. Porter was downstairs, and it was only a couple times a year that the whole mill took off, and the night before was the only night that everybody would be fixing to not work the next day, which can lead to some problems. There was liquor down at the Point, like everywhere else, as folks had it tucked away here and there. Word was that the rumrunners even put in right at the Point at night, but this I have never seen, although with all the creeks around here, it is not hard to picture.

With the celebrating coming on the Fourth, booze would surely be around on the evening of the third. Porter knew this as well as anybody, so on nights like these he was a little jumpy, expecting a problem that he couldn't put his finger on. I stayed away from the stuff as it has done me no service.

Anyways, back to Thursday night. Stanley walked home with me, and we made arrangements for him to come by the boarding house after he'd had supper with Helen and the kids. Invitations to eat with Stanley's family were not being extended by Helen at this particular time.

I went home and walked up the stairs and got a good washing in the bathroom, getting the grit off pretty well. I had some summer sausage stored up and took it with some water and some of the hard bread that I could get at the little bakery just up from the company store. The water softened it up a bit, and with the sausage it makes for a nice meal.

About 7:00 I walked back down to the lobby, picked up a newspaper that was sitting on the table at the front door, and made my way over to the little sitting area that they penned us in. It wasn't a lobby like you might picture at a hotel, the tables and chairs being dirty in spots and shabby, but it was good enough, and there were a couple rockers, and Porter would open the windows up since there were screens. We didn't have them on the second floor, and downstairs they kept the bugs out pretty good.

Porter had an icebox at the counter, and in it he would keep cold sodas that you could buy for three cents apiece. It was his little branch of the company store right there at the front desk. After Stanley arrived, we made our way over to Porter and bought a couple. I picked up Stanley's because, with working at the stadium and not having any kids, I knew I had a little more spare change than him generally.

"That will be six cents, Henry," Porter said.

"Thanks Porter. This here's Stanley. He works with me at the belt, and he's run out on his family for the night to join us boys down here for a pop."

Porter turned to Stanley, "I know Mr. Sowa, Henry. Stanley, how is the married life?"

"It's good Porter. I wouldn't get too fixed on it, though, with your nose," Stanley laughed.

I preferred me poking fun at Porter to other folks doing it.

"Well Stanley, you've managed, and you lived here on the first floor for several years, so that means its open to anyone, I believe," Porter answered.

That was that and Stanley and me pulled up a couple chairs to a table in the lobby and set into our sodas. I was telling him that according to the *Sun* the Toronto Maple Leafs were in town playing the Orioles. It was always interesting to me having a team coming all the way down from Canada to face our boys.

Let me say the Orioles weren't what they was a couple years ago. They won their league five straight times including last year, but I am not so sure they will pull it off again. The first time they won it, I was still living up at Camp Upton, but by 1921 I was down here, and I do believe that may have been their best team yet. I have gone out to a ballgame a couple times, but not up in Baltimore. On Sundays they wasn't allowed to play in the city so old Jack Dunn, their owner, would bring them down to play at Back River Park, which was not far from here at all.

One time they even had soldier's day at Back River, and I pulled on my uniform and as a direct result got in for free, which will make you enjoy almost any ballgame. That afternoon Dunnie had Jack Bentley pitching, and he polished off Syracuse like it was no trouble. They called old Jack the minor league Babe Ruth because he could hit and pitch, but now that he's back in the big leagues, I suppose that will have to change.

Anyway, there were about six other fellows sitting around playing cards or what have you at the tables near ours. I found that when I had a newspaper with me and Stanley and Reginald around, they tended to let me pick it up and do the reading. Now I can tell Reginald can read a few things because he says, "Turn left" after he sees a sign that says to turn or something similar, but I am not sure Stanley can. His folks are from what I would call Russia, but if you look on a map now it will say Poland, and I don't think he ever learned English right when he got here as a kid. At the Point they make a pretty big deal out of everybody learning to read if they can, but as you can understand, there are times where a kid can probably fake it and a teacher might not even tell, or if they could they just was quiet about it, knowing that the kid was going to be working at the mill.

So I would read straight away. I am not half bad, and tonight Stanley listened closely, and I set him straight on where the Orioles were on July 3, 1924, in the standings. This got us talking about sports, and after awhile we got to talking about football a little and the stadium. Stanley knew I was working Sundays but didn't say much about it at the mill.

"They paying you and Reginald pretty good up there?" he asked, looking down at the table like he wasn't asking at all.

I paused and looked over at Porter. He was taking stock of his soda inventory.

"I don't know about Reginald—you know he hardly says much—but I'm making out okay. If I add it on top of what I'm making at the mill, I have a little to spare for the sodas."

He lowered his voice. "You feel funny getting a job from a colored boy?"

I sat and sipped my soda and thought about what Stanley thought "funny" was. I knew what he meant, of course; here at the Point that type of thing just would not happen, no matter what. They ran the town and ran how people walked through it, start to finish.

"It's work and you know Reginald. I work with his father. A real gentleman."

Let me say I have seen a man next to me run through with a bayonet. They did not eye each other to see what color they was before they did it. They just killed and that was that. The 92nd was in the Argonne, and as you know, they was colored. They held up better than the French when things got hot, and you can write that down. I saw the 92nd fight alongside the French so this is not a guess.

"They need anyone else?" Stanley asked.

This was another tough one because Stanley wasn't a fellow that you wanted to recommend too highly, if you know what I mean. Probably wouldn't help your job standing at that particular place.

"Me and Reginald and his father pretty much have the place covered," I answered with a laugh.

He gave up on it.

The Orioles had beat Toronto yesterday, 8-3. Rube Parnham shut down the Maple Leafs and Fritz Maisel hit a homer to seal it. The *Sun* could make you feel like you was at the game, the way they told it.

After reading through the big stuff and getting to little stories like how butter is sometimes made right in Baltimore even though you might think it was from way out in the country, Stanley started yawning, and I was even getting a little bored with my reading.

"Alright Stanley. Helen's probably back home worrying about you, so you should probably be getting back there."

It was not late, but I didn't mind the idea of getting into bed early if I was going to be heading over to Bay Shore the next day.

"Right. Time for me to get going. You have a good day tomorrow, Henry. You working up at the stadium?"

He said it a little too loudly, and Porter just looked over this way while acting like he really wasn't looking over this way.

"Sorry," Stanley said, now all whispery.

"No, I'm off like everybody else."

I said this and then gave Porter a big smile to show him I knew he was listening. His head shot down again like him properly counting those sodas was keeping world politics in place.

With that, Stanley was out the door. I headed up to bed and sure enough had one of the awful dreams of which I have made tell. It being July, I awoke soaked through my shirt again. I opened the window, knowing full well I might awake under a covering of soot, but there was no way around it.

CHAPTER 8

The Point always put on a nice show for the Fourth, with a big parade down D Street, that being the main street, of sorts, for the town. But unless you are a kid or have some, there comes a time when one parade starts to look like another. On D Street this happens pretty quick because the same groups are always in it. The fire department is always the big show because there is a lot of wood at the Point and they can easily convince you that what they do is pretty important, which it is. For the parade they might put a sign on the truck that says, "A single match can destroy a city," and show somebody's mom crying next to a burning city. This is not entirely correct in this modern age, but I suppose it is done to keep kids from fooling with matches, so the idea is a good one. The other big float is usually put together by the mill, and last year it said, "Steel Means Progress." You can see that if you've watched this a few years, you are pretty well set for keeps.

I got myself into the hallway shower on Saturday before most of the boys was up. A lot of them were laying in late, taking the time to sleep without any church like some of them might have on a Sunday, although our house did not break any records for attending church. By 8:00 I was on my way out the door to the trolley stop that stood just up the road from our building. Before I made it out, Porter, who I do not believe sleeps, sure enough was there to register my action on the list of things that Porter notices.

"No work today, Henry, but out you go, the early bird."

"The worm's at Bay Shore Park, Porter."

I'm not sure why, but I winked. Porter was like a teacher. You felt guilty around him sometimes for no reason. But I was past and the screen door snapped back at my heels.

"Say hi to the ladies, Henry!" was the last thing I heard from the house.

The trolley service away from the Point towards the park was never real heavy. I had to make sure I caught the 8:20 because otherwise there was nothing until 9:00. The train was peaceful and quiet. The Point does have its nice days, like I said, depending on the smoke, and on the Fourth the stacks were off and it was clear and a little cooler now than it would be later in the day. It's hard to work at a steel mill and say something was perfect, but right now, after three months of working straight, I was sitting down and feeling perfect.

The ride was short and at some point a family came on board and then another, and the funny thing about both was the kids was already in their swim trunks. When we got near the park, they got real quiet, and when we passed under that rollercoaster, there was a thundering whoosh from above that I was not expecting. Sure enough a coaster car had passed over us right as we pulled in. The families started clapping, and then a little boy turned back to me to see if I was clapping, too. Truth was that car rushing over us had me nearly on the floor, I am ashamed to say. He peered down at me with a funny look on his face, a little scared. I got up from my crouching and started clapping real quick like I was just pretend ducking for a gag. The boy brightened up and damned if he didn't wink at me and started clapping louder.

The thing about Bay Shore that you might not know is that they really put a lot of work into it for the customers. First there was the main house, with its balconies, that was right near where you got off the trolley. I call it a house, but it was a restaurant, and it was like a picture. It sounds funny when talking about a restaurant, but it is true. It had a porch on top and bottom. On the outside it was all fancied up with a sign that said "Seafood Supper $1.00" right in front of the top windows, which was kind of nice to know up front before you walked in what dinner was going to cost you. It would be nice if more restaurants did that sort of thing.

Out in front of that was a fountain, and the kids from the trolley ran straight towards it and got their heads wet like they'd done it a hundred times. The same boy that saw me ducking asked his father for a penny to throw in, but times as they were, his father just looked down and then looked over at me like he'd done something wrong. Then the kid looked down at the ground and found a little stone.

"Make a wish, mama!" he shouted and then let the stone go, and it hit the fountain and shot straight back out at him.

He was a tough little character and picked it right up and threw it back, getting two wishes out of the same stone, which of course beats throwing a penny in there for one.

I wandered around and saw families like that a lot, going here and there, nobody much in a hurry and just taking things in. Over on the side of the trolley station there was a long pier called the Crystal Pier that headed way out into the bay. We see plenty of piers down at the Point, but they are mostly for unloading ore. As I walked out, the breeze kicked up from the north, and on the sides were some fishermen leaning over the rails. Going up and down were lots of people just thrilled to be out and feeling the breeze. One boy decided to ride his bike out until a policeman chased him off, and we all laughed, and even the policeman didn't seem too mad, it being the Fourth of July.

The day slowly passed on, and I won't write it all the way through because if you have been to an amusement park, you have an idea of how it might go. I spent a little extra, just this once, on peanuts from a man roasting some back near the trolley barn, and it was well worth the little something. I bought a lemonade for the peanuts after they nearly salted my mouth dry and then sat right down near the rollercoaster on a little bench. If you watch a rollercoaster, it's funny to see how everybody screams at about the same time, but by the time they were done, they were almost always smiling.

Occasionally something would fly off and hit the ground, and just while I was sitting there a watch, a necklace, and some pennies came flying down. I began to think a fellow could make a pretty good living sitting under a rollercoaster, but then I looked over, and there was a policeman on a bench just across from me, and sure enough he would walk under and put everything that fell in a little metal container with a handle. When the ride was over, he'd walk over to where everybody got off, and they'd have a little chat.

He waited and held back the can and then would talk to the people, ask them a few things without letting them see in, and then if they answered, he handed it to them, and it was smiles all around. I can't figure out what they did about the pennies each time, for anyone can say they lost a penny and it has Lincoln on it and it is round and flat. But I suppose it all worked out. He made a lot of people happy just by giving them back what was already theirs.

The lemonade and peanuts only made a dent in my hunger, so I started thinking about the restaurant and going back and forth as a man will to himself on whether he should buy an expensive meal. I decided to go ahead.

Living as I did upstairs at the Point, I chose the first floor for my supper. They had this long table running along the side windows for people having a meal with just themselves. A dollar was a lot for me, but I hadn't had a rockfish at a restaurant in my life, and there they were on the menu, so this was special. I ordered myself a Coca-Cola this time and had the rockfish and the cola (with ice) and even some cole slaw and a big fat biscuit covered with butter that melted down right as I was getting it.

If this was not good enough, I had a piece of cake that they said was the sort made over on Smith Island. I had no idea where that was, but it was the biggest I'd ever seen, so they must be a happy bunch down in those parts.

The lights was on outside now, and this is where Bay Shore really got to be something special. Electric lights aren't new anymore, but when they lit up the park there must have been a few thousand or more, and they ran right out along the pier, and later on tonight the bay would look like the sky with all the lights reflecting off it. Just like on the trolley car, the people clapped, this time for the lights coming on. A couple of the older French soldiers who could speak English told us a little about the World's Fair when we was over there, and from what they said I imagine it was something like this pier.

Since it was a first rate operation they have at Bay Shore, after the cake I was offered a cup of coffee. It was steaming hot and served in a fine china mug, no tin here. I sipped it down as properly as I could. I looked up at the waitress who kind of smiled to show me I was doing it right. She told me the coffee came from somewhere in the Amazon and was sent here direct. Bay Shore is like that.

CHAPTER 9

Saturday passed and after describing Bay Shore, writing about the mill would be like writing about a rock after talking about a mountain—not a lot of point to it. On Sunday it was back up to the stadium with Reginald on the trolley, and I had a lot to say about Bay Shore, and he listened and nodded and asked a few things about the food.

"Good coffee?"

"Top of the line. They are not fooling around down there when it comes to supper."

I asked him about what he'd done, and he said he'd been up at the city with his folks and they'd set out on the porch and the neighbors lit off some fireworks that, as it turned out, burned down a shed right behind their house. I wondered if he was being showy just to keep up with my Bay Shore story.

"Burned it down from fireworks? They have gasoline on them or something?"

Which I found quite amusing and laughed about, but Reginald does not laugh at a lot of the good ones I tell.

"No, some things burn without gasoline, which you'd know if you'd paid attention more."

"Paid attention to what?"

Then I started laughing more and for once, the sixth of July, I got Reginald Spector laughing, too. His old man laughed more than him, come to think of it, which was irregular, older folks generally having had things rougher than their children.

* * *

The following Sunday we were finishing up for the day. The weather in July in Baltimore bakes up pretty warmly, and Mr. Spector and I were awfully tired after having nearly all the water sweated out of us.

We got to the top of the stadium when it hit 4 o'clock and we were done working, and just sat down. The sun was still pretty high, and the heat had not let up. We each had a shovel, and Mr. Spector had a hand trowel and a little rake that he worked like a wand on some of the patches. It was a handful for an old man to carry after a long day.

"Where do you keep these, Mr. Spector?" I asked.

"On the far side of the bleachers in a little shed marked 'Tools.' You walked past it ten times now since you been here," he said.

Proving to him I was more observant than your average worker, I grabbed the tools from him and just said, "You're tired. I'll take them across. Have a rest."

I didn't wait for a reply because Mr. Spector liked things a certain way and didn't always give you a shot at doing it some other way. You'd be pretty surprised how much a man could want a hole of dirt filled in just so, but it is possible. I was off in a hurry before he could stop me.

The top of the stadium was like a ridge, if you can picture that, and everybody moved along the top of the ridge unless you broke off down one of the stairwells to get to the field below or out of the stadium along the side. For a short stretch you tucked under the upper bleachers with all the truss work, and then there was a little break between bleacher sections, and that was the spot Mr. Spector was talking about. I'd seen it often enough, I imagine, just never fixed on it.

Now Mr. Spector took this path every day, I am sure, to get those tools back to where they belonged. But me, I was hardly ever up there this time of day. When I walked through the shadows mixed with the shifting sunlight under the bleachers, I noticed it lit on some hay tucked under the upper section. In with the hay was wooden crates, but they only poked out in a couple spots, so if you didn't look too closely, you might not see them. It was sensible enough to have some bales of hay up there, as they could be used to soak up a puddle in a hurry after a rain, but the crates looked almost like they was being hidden by the hay because they were half-tucked in it. Like your mom hiding Christmas presents under the rug, it looked funny and didn't make much sense.

I was looking over at the hay when all of a sudden I ran into somebody and fell backward at the blow that caught me right in the eye and had me seeing stars. I went to the ground hard, and my head hit the dirt and snapped back up. I was shook for a moment and laid there. When I got my bearings, I got up to my elbows, looked over at another fellow on the ground, and said, "You alright?"

There was no answer. He must've been running, I thought, for us to bang heads like that. I held the corner of my eye, that hard bony part just to the outside of it, and it smarted when I touched it.

"You alright?" I asked again, figuring maybe this fellow was in the same shape as me.

"I'm fine. Where were you looking that you run smack into a guy?"

I wasn't running, I'll point out. If anyone was, it was this fellow.

"This is my first time through at this hour. I was bringing the tools back. I looked away for a minute and I saw the crates over there."

With that, he stood up, and I could see now who it was, a fellow named Russell who worked on the new bleachers most of the time, so I didn't have much occasion to talk to him.

He looked at me.

"Dawson, any crates you see over there you're imagining. You been out in the sun too long today."

This was a strange comment.

"They're right over there, Russell. You're the one out in the sun too long."

I dusted off and when I looked up, Russell was a few feet closer.

"Like I said, Dawson, there's nothing over there. You tell Spector to bring his own damn tools back next time."

Now him acting this way was slowly adding up. More than once in my time I'd come across somebody who has a box of some sort that he decides you didn't see, and if you did see, it was empty. At Camp Upton there were boys all over who had these boxes once Prohibition kicked in.

"Sure Russell, he's old and will be sure to give a brave fellow and his crates a wide path. You're right, those crates ain't there and they probably ain't full of booze, either. And we didn't just knock heads, either."

I didn't wait to hear what he had to say next because that was meant to agitate him and not to keep the conversation oiled. I just picked up the tools and kept walking.

About 20 yards past Russell, I found the shed. I opened it up, and it was as tidy as a pin on the inside. There were wooden pegs along the walls that jutted out a good deal and each one had initials on top of them. Most had been crossed out a couple of times, but the one that said H.S. on it had only ever had his initials, you could see straightaway. I put the tools into their proper spot, took a look around to get a better feel for the place, then stepped out and closed up behind me.

I was back under the bleachers, keeping my eyes open so I wouldn't have another run-in with Russell. He must have got off to somewhere, which was fine with me.

"Tools back okay, Henry?" Mr. Spector asked, sitting down with his back turned to me and not giving me a full once over when I returned.

"They're back okay. Let's head down," I answered and started walking towards the ramp.

After a few steps, he caught a look at my eye.

"Henry! You walk into a post under those bleachers?"

He took out his dirty old rag and immediately pushed it up against the corner of my eye.

"A post named Russell," I muttered looking at the ground.

He pushed harder on the towel and let me tell you it smarted.

"Henry, Russell is a foul-tempered man, and most everybody knows that, and I guess you just finding out. What they got under them bleachers is no business of mine or yours, unless we want to lose our jobs. I worked too hard for that."

It was not that easy for me, especially since I just took one in the eye.

"With us working hard all day long, it's not right he's running booze right here. You know it isn't. Why don't he keep it in an old boarded up place, someplace nobody's getting all fixed up for the President?" I said.

I knew the answer without asking. Hiding booze where you was gonna use it was usually easier than trying to sneak it there when you wanted to. I'd seen that before, too.

He didn't say anymore, just took the old rag off my eye, folded it like it was the queen's linen, and put it back into his overalls.

We came down the ramp and Reginald spotted my eye, and to his credit did not fuss about it.

"The 26 is coming. Let's get moving," he said.

We got on the trolley and didn't say much, but Reginald seemed bothered and wouldn't let on. I don't know how much he guessed about what had happened, but whatever his guess was, he was content with it.

Reginald got off the trolley on his side of the Humphrey's Creek clearing, and then we was moving again.

Porter was the opposite of the Spectors. If he found something unusual or bothersome or aggravating or interesting, he just got louder.

"Henry, what's wrong with your eye?" he shouted at me when I walked in.

There was one other sort of scraggly looking fellow in the lobby, but it being a Sunday and him being off, he was out cold asleep in a rocking chair facing the front of the house. This was the type of socializing the mill set you up for after six days of work.

"Nothing, Porter, just some tough luck. I'll go wash it up."

"My tough luck doesn't get me a black eye, Henry. Especially on my day off from work. That sounds like luck you can change."

I let it stand as there was nothing to say back. It would just worsen things, and my head was hurting, so I might as well just keep walking. I got up to the hall bathroom quickly and locked the door behind me. It was a double bathroom, so I usually did not do this, but I didn't want anyone wandering in. I reached for the tiny cord dangling from the light bulb above the sink.

Damn. I looked bad, like what Jack Dempsey must look like after an off night, except with some dirt mixed in for good measure. I wet down a towel pretty good then dabbed at it. I was cut and I needed to get the dirt out. It was throbbing now, and I can see how the champ earns his dough.

CHAPTER 10

"It's worse now, Henry."

That was how I started my day. I knew it looked worse, I just came from the bathroom, and this mug is nothing to start a day with on a good day, but today it was particularly alarming.

"Give it time, Porter," was the best I could do.

I missed Reginald and Stanley on the walk in and just fell in with an older fellow named Leznick who kept to himself most days. He worked in the coke ovens and didn't give you much to think of him other than he could have a distinct odor come the end of a work day in the ovens. This was to be expected, but still the stench was powerful enough to surprise you at times.

But this morning he got a look at the eye, and it livened him up a bit, especially with nothing but the coke oven waiting at the end of his walk.

"Dunnie's got the Orioles looking good. Boley hit one out Saturday," he said, a little jittery and starting in straight with baseball.

He's not half-bad this Leznick, looking at a guy with an egg for an eye and talking about the Orioles.

"I missed it. Who'd they beat?"

"Newark. The Bears."

"Well good. Knowing Dunnie, he's paying Boley about the same as me."

Truth was Dunnie paid the boys pretty well. It just broke you up seeing them leave for the big leagues, so you felt you had to complain just to explain it happening.

I'll spare you the part about Reginald seeing the eye again, for you have already got a good feel for it if you were listening when I was talking about the trolley ride. Stanley had a look, and I can only guess what he thought because he didn't let on when he saw it. Before long the belt was moving, and we weren't talking about much of anything at all.

* * *

Mrs. Foss was working at the bank when I stopped in on Monday night to drop off another check from the city of Baltimore. I tried to avoid her, what with the shouting and my eye and another one of my yellow checks—it would have been trouble for certain.

But sure enough there was only two lines, and for a reason I can guess they doubled up on the line that was next to Mrs. Foss, and there was her line without a person in it.

I looked at the floor for a minute, hoping for something to come up, I do not know what, when she called, "Henry!"

That was that, then. I could get the shouting up close or get it across the bank lobby. I scooted up quick to the little cage in front of her and gave her my check.

"That eye is as big as an antler!" she shouted. With that, the sweat started on the back of my neck a little like it will at times now.

"Just one!" I shouted back and then gave her a little wink at the same time with the good eye and pushed the check forward to get her looking down, not up.

"I'll say, but as big as two!" she yelled and laughed but kept her hands working on the paperwork to deposit the check.

"The usual?" she asked.

"Same as ever. Thank you."

She gave me back my $1.50. She also passed me a little note that said how much was in my account. She took her job seriously and didn't shout out the numbers unless she had too, which was not often.

There was now over $40 to my name, and in its way, having that between me and living out on the street made me feel a little more established in life. Truth was, working at Venable hadn't yet changed my life much, but as you saw the bank account go up, I now started feeling a possibility that it might change.

* * *

One day we got to talking as fellows will up at the stadium.

"How's Reginald like it here?" I asked Mr. Spector.

He was shoveling some sand over a bare spot right at the very top of the slope on the eastern side of Venable. He didn't hear me, so I said it again.

"I'm not sure, Henry, you two fellows work together. How's he say he likes it?"

This was a good question, but Reginald never really talked about working here. A couple of reasons for that will jump out at you. First is with the belt moving you don't talk much, as I've said. Second, it is best to keep quiet about moonlighting while still at your day job.

"We don't talk about it at the mill. It doesn't come up."

He kept working, and I threw some sand into a spot that needed tending.

"Henry, you two are two of a kind. Now I don't talk too much, and I know it, and that's about that. But you two got the world ahead of you, and far as I can figure, you don't mention nothing but the weather. And you working here, for instance. I'm glad to have you, but how you supposed to socialize with the girls if you working seven days a week? Tell me that."

I had no answer. My order of important things was to make a few extra dollars so you have something to ask a gal out with before you did the asking. Before I was working here, I couldn't have asked a gal to go out for a glass of milk with me, it was that tight.

"Well, I'm saving some money here to ask a girl out with."

"Yeah, and when are you going to go out if you don't have a day off?"

I shifted around some dirt into the right spot and then patted it down with my shovel.

"I haven't gotten there yet, and when I do, I'll let you know."

He was not done. Funny, Mr. Spector was like a spigot in some ways when it came to talking. On or off.

"You ever talk to women, Henry? Working at a mill and a stadium don't exactly have you rubbing elbows with ladies every day of the week."

I had no answer again. There was Mrs. Foss I talked to pretty regular, but that was not anything beyond how much I wanted to put in the bank. That was not romantic talk.

"Some," I replied, which was no lie but not all of the truth, either.

"Some. Um hum. Reginald probably got the same sharp plan you have for waiting to meet a lady. I tell you, if I thought like you or him before I was courting Mrs. Spector, there would have been no courting, no marrying, and no Reginald!"

He then picked up the bucket of sand and trudged a little farther up the hill. I followed but didn't throw out anything more because he seemed to have an answer for everything I said, with room to spare.

"I tell you, Henry, just think about it once in awhile. You work hard as anyone, but you know things don't just happen on their own. You got to decide to make them happen. Now let's keep going," he said and walked up the hill.

CHAPTER 11

The next time that I will point something out about Venable was late September. We got through the summer okay, the Orioles won the pennant again, their sixth in a row I should add, and I was still working my full seven days a week. I could tell you more about what went on at the mill during that time, but nothing jumps out at me too much, and I could say about the same for the past three years if I talk it all the way through. It was a mill job, and if you didn't get injured and you got your paycheck, those were the highlights and you were thankful to have them. The boys down at the mill worked hard and I considered myself fortunate to have lodging among them, but we as a group did not veer too much from what we was doing day to day.

I did not make it out to Bay Shore again but I would have liked to. I would see the folks going off in the other direction to the park on Sunday when I took the train up to Venable, and part of me always wanted to join them. One thing I should point out is that in the fall the bugs begin to clear out from the Point and, smell or not or smoke or not, it definitely moves up a grade if you are rating it as a place in general.

Things kept going along at Venable like they needed to with the park coming into shape. They kept adding extra seats for the big game, and by this time the upper section was nearly complete and rising up from the original seats. The stadium stood out more against the sky with everything below almost all blocked out save for a few trees. It smelled like a pine forest in there some days with all the cutting and all the trimmings on the ground. I would be away for a week and then come back, and it was nice to look around and see what had been built up while I was away.

As the game got closer, they had me working on a fence that ran along the top of the slope down to the field, and then on the other side of the walkway there was another fence that kept people from falling backwards down the slope towards the outside of the stadium.

It seems like nothing, fixing a fence, but there was a lot of it, and I got myself work almost all the way around the park setting it right. One morning, which I will make only quick mention of, I leaned too hard on a post that I was setting in place and it gave way. I rolled down the hill at a good clip for about thirty feet, and then Mr. Spector came running down after me and lost his footing, and a second later I was keeping him from going down the rest of the hill on a roll. We both ended up fine, and compared to some ends that fellows met at the mill when things went badly, we were damn lucky.

Mr. Spector was good at working the fence, and I could see why they like him at Venable. He could do a lot of things pretty good, not just a couple. The more time I worked with him, the more I saw he worked this place like it was his own. There was always stuff tipping over or blowing down or washing away, and he would show up in the morning, and we'd just go about setting things straight. He could look up and see things to fix right off.

On an afternoon in early fall, and this was particularly exciting, we were allowed to walk across the top of the entrance to the stadium to get from one side to the other. This may not sound like much, but it sure cut down on the walking, and when I was strolling along the top with the columns underneath and the city spread out in front, you could almost picture yourself going off to sign the Armistice or something that important. Of course we wasn't, but it felt that way.

As it would happen, this same day that I was allowed to cut across the top of the entrance, and I should add Mr. Spector never said why we was allowed, Hadley Overman spotted me from where he was out towards 33rd Street. He was looking over the entrance, and there we was walking right along the top of it.

"Dawson!" I heard shouted from below.

I immediately flopped onto my stomach, thinking I was in the soup, and I can say a man who has been in the war can hit the dirt quicker than most. Mr. Spector stopped walking and looked down at me.

"Henry, get your tail up. He seen you, otherwise he would have yelled, 'Hey, you!' not 'Dawson!' You look silly. Get on up."

He had a point. I was found out before I dove down.

I got up and brushed off, trying to make it look like I slipped at the very moment that Overman had shouted my name. I do not think he bought the notion.

"Dawson, come on down. I want to talk to you in my office," he said.

"Yes, sir!" I shouted and I started to give him a little salute and then caught myself and held it back.

I looked at Mr. Spector, and he knew what I was thinking.

"Don't worry Henry, it ain't because we up here. I was told yesterday that it's getting closer to the big game, and we're allowed to walk along this rooftop if it will get us back and forth between the sides quicker," he said.

This was a little comforting, knowing at least now why we were allowed to do it. So I finished off our walk to the far side with Mr. Spector, and then I headed down the ramp.

We had been walking to get at a sandy patch that opened up into a little ravine on the front left of the stadium. If you didn't get at it early, it would spread quickly, and this one was beginning to.

I walked in through that front door of the Administration Building and made my turn into what was now a familiar place, but not exactly comfortable. I knocked on his door, the same one I'd come through on my first day.

I walked in and there was Overman sitting behind his desk. There was a man that I couldn't make out sitting in a chair in front of his desk, and then there was one more chair with nobody in it. The man in the first chair had on a coat with a mink collar, which you don't really need in Baltimore in September, but I suppose if you buy such a coat you might be eager to use it.

"Dawson, come in. This, as I'm sure you know, is Mayor Jackson."

Well, hell, I didn't know because although I look at the *Sun*, a fellow looks a lot different in person than flat and black and white on a paper. And on any particular day, I do not think that I am about to walk in on the mayor himself. This was exciting in its way but more than a little alarming. I could not think of a thing on God's green earth that the mayor would want to talk to me about, so I got a little nervous, as you might guess. The room did a funny wavy thing for just a second, which was okay because it came and just passed through and then I started walking toward the desk and Mr. Mayor.

"Dawson, Mayor Jackson. Mr. Mayor, this is Henry Dawson. He works on the stadium for us once a week."

"Pleased to meet you finally, Dawson," he said while rising to shake my hand.

"Finally" sounded a little funny coming from a mayor about me.

"It is my pleasure, Mr. Mayor. This city is a real square deal," I said.

That makes no particular sense, but out it came.

"Dawson," Hadley Overman said, "it's come to my attention that you were involved very directly in the fighting in the Argonne."

It came to his attention when it came out of my mouth. He was playing at something for the mayor, putting on a formal voice like you might at a banquet, if you can understand that.

"Yes, sir."

"A look at your service record," he held up some papers, "indicates that you were a member of the Lost Battalion."

I looked at my hands. Now I knew where we might be going. This had happened before, including down at the Point before a Fourth of July parade. I had to do some fast talking back then. They wanted me to get on the fireman's float and put out a fake fire with my army uniform on, which was plain stupid, and I hated the idea of being in a parade just for not getting shot.

"Yes sir," I said and kept looking at my hands.

The mayor then cut in.

"I understand you were directly involved in the fighting in the Pocket, Dawson. We are all proud."

I very directly killed men when they was pushing into the Pocket and have seen them die directly. One boy began crying right as I was killing him. This will tear you up.

"Yes, sir."

"We've found three other men who were in the Lost Battalion who are living here in Maryland," Overman said.

I said nothing. I could not guess his point exactly, but because of the Fourth of July parade I guessed what it might be. Lead the Army team in a charge out onto the field with my bayonet fixed or something of that high order.

Overman continued, "At the football game we'd like to celebrate your bravery, Dawson. It would look well before the President and the other dignitaries for Maryland to have four of our finest representing the city and the state. We were hoping to have a little ceremony as part of the halftime show," he said.

I did not know what to say, and my hands were sweating now. I nodded.

Hadley took a little notice of my feeling out of sorts and himself looked unsettled, but the mayor was considering the caretaking of the city in the back of his head and seemed as pleased as can be with this discussion.

"Dawson," said Hadley, "the other three men that we'd like to have join you are Private Frank Duncan, Private Michael Lynch, and Sergeant Norman Carr."

"Lynch is dead, sir," I said.

Overman looked at the mayor, surprised.

"Are you sure?"

Lynch was shot through the chest next to me. I could fit my fist into the hole that opened up in his back. He bled to death on top of me while I sat there like a bastard and told him he was going to be fine. Lynch died with me saying that very thing.

"Yes, sir."

I held the chair with my right hand. It felt like it was going to go slide backward on me any minute. I clenched it with all my might. Since I got back home, I could get that unsettled without deciding to, real quick.

"Well…" Overman said, looking at the mayor.

"Well," he started up again, "We'll have Private Duncan and Sergeant Carr there, and the three of you can march out at halftime. The mayor would like to present you with the city's battle medal."

"Yes, sir," I said yet again. I could not think of more. I wanted to just get out and be back on the slope, working.

Then, the mayor stood up, looked at Overman, looked at me, and extended his hand.

"Well Private Dawson, it has been my pleasure. I looked forward to seeing you on the 29th of November then."

He nodded towards Hadley and then walked towards the door without another word. You could hear his shoes echoing down the long hallway to the front of the building.

My grip loosed on the chair. Hadley cleared his throat.

"Thank you, Dawson. Everything alright then?"

I turned towards him. Some relief was working its way in.

"Yes, Mr. Overman. Thank you."

"Everything okay with the job? I heard there was a misunderstanding about where some tools went under the bleachers. You know where they go now, correct?"

I looked up slowly.

"Yes, sir. Mr. Spector takes them back now, sir. He's got his favorite spot and his favorite way. He only looks straight ahead. Not under the bleachers."

He raised his eyebrow at this like that was a little less clear than what he was hoping to hear.

"Well, if it's your turn, you'll know where they belong and where they don't belong," he said. "They don't belong under the bleachers, if I'm making myself understood. We will be fully hosting some important people at the game, and the city has obligations concerning their entertainment in the days leading up to the event. Weather permitting, we'll be hosting a dance here on the eve of the game for some of the local football aficionados."

I paused for a moment and breathed deep to steady up a little. I began in again.

"I'll be plain with you, Mr. Overman. I don't know everything that goes on under the bleachers, but I'm certain it's not hammering nails all day."

He looked at me, then looked around like there was somebody in the room who might hear us when there wasn't, and leaned his head in.

"Dawson, I'm not absolutely certain of what you're talking about, but you would do well to make a few considerations. Foremost is that the best way to remain employed at Venable is to comply with our rules, whether or not they are written down. And they are not all written down. Also, you'd do well to consider this is 1924 and not everything that you might take exception to would be something that others would. Our governor for one. Mr. Mencken for another."

I can stand with Governor Ritchie doing what he thought was best for the state and speaking out against Prohibition. But, well, Mencken is an ass, and his writing about drinking so freely just makes me wish a revenue agent would toss him in the lockup and grab his pen from him while doing it.

"Mr. Overman, all I will say is that fellows have worked a lot harder to bring this place along than I have, and I understand that. It's something you can look at and feel proud of, and it's not a medal that's going to sit in a box somewhere. It's something that anyone can walk into and see and think that Baltimore is something on its own. Not just a train station you pass through from New York to Washington. And here we are right in the middle of it, right in the center, with this liquor. It's embarrassing with all we're doing here. With all the work you're doing here yourself you have to see that."

Overman looked at me. He then pushed up his glasses from the tip of his nose and looked down at some papers like that was what he'd been doing all along until this unpleasant conversation started up.

"That is a good speech for a temperance tent, Dawson, but here it will get you fired. And let me be clear, it will get you fired quickly, and it will not reflect well on our employees who recommended you for this position either. Consider that. Good evening."

When I was back outdoors, and thankful to be, the first person I saw was Mr. Spector. He was milling around, pretending like he wasn't milling around.

"You fired, Henry?" he asked straight away. "No, I'm not fired."

"Well, you something, because it don't take Mr. Overman and the mayor himself to tell you nothing is going on, now does it? Shoot, it doesn't take the mayor to fire you, neither, come to think of it."

"I'm in the halftime show at the game. I was in the Argonne, Mr. Spector. They want to make a fuss about it. I suppose the servicemen will like it."

He laughed.

"What a fuss that you ain't dead? Well, have them talk to me. I'll tell them that not only are you not dead, but you are alive and still having a go at fellows whenever you get a chance to take some tools back to the shed. That's just what I would tell them, too."

He then laughed some more like he had just let go with about the funniest thing a guy could come up with. I was not in a joking mood.

CHAPTER 12

Although I did not let on about it, Mr. Spector's words to me about not taking the time to meet a girl settled in. Like I said to him, the only woman that I saw regular was Mrs. Foss at the bank, and I never thought about asking her out on a date until me and Mr. Spector got to talking.

Besides not having any money until I started working at Venable, Mrs. Foss still went by "Mrs." even though she was not officially married to Mr. Foss anymore with him being killed. I didn't normally think of a "Mrs." as being in the courting category. Plus, with her working at the bank, you were always handing money back and forth or talking about money, and it kept the conversation in a limited area, especially if there happened to be a line behind me. With her bad hearing and loud talking, on the chance I did ask her out, I would have to shout it. If she said "No!" well, that would be awfully loud coming out from her, and I would certainly regret having done it.

These things kept a lid on any romantic ideas I might have, and to be honest, I didn't have much of any until lately. Like I said, Mrs. Foss was a pretty woman. Hearing her shout was not a pretty thing, but if you looked past that you could see that she was. She was not tall, but she had nice brown hair pinned up, real bright cheeks and brown eyes. She was easy with the smile, which always makes a woman look prettier.

Her husband, Wilton Foss, I never knew, but I heard tell around the mill that he was an ornery fellow.

Once he was killed in battle, you don't want to point that out too much, so people would say something like, "Wilton was killed at Chateau Thierry. What a terrible thing." Then they might have a little pause long enough to let you know they'd said something nice about a dead doughboy, and then they would let slip, "With all the fighting he did here regular at the Point, I think he was all fought out by the time he got over there."

So if you compare me to an ornery guy like Wilton, you will be pretty pleased, for I do not agitate too easily. Mix in Mrs. Foss being pretty in a way you might not notice, and that she was the only gal that I could count on seeing regular, and you might have an idea about a date. At least I did.

After making up my mind to ask her out, I took to putting together a plan for a date that was straightforward enough. On Friday she would be working late, with the bank staying open until six and all. I could try to be one of the last boys in there with my check and then could ask her for a walk home. If I timed it out right, the line would have moved on through, and I could do this without too much notice if the asking did not got well.

As Friday rolled in, I followed through on it pretty good. There wasn't much to say to Stanley and Reginald because they didn't usually put their check in the bank on Friday nights, maybe holding off through the weekend so the money wouldn't disappear too quickly on them. So it was just me like always, and with the evening whistle blowing at 5:30, I had time to stop down in one of the mill bathrooms and wash off my face a little bit. The bathrooms at the mill, as you can guess, were grimy, so I said "See you" to the boys and got to work in there.

The soap was gone, which was pretty usual, so I had planned ahead and slipped a little in my pocket from home for just that reason. I got most of the dirt off my face and wet back my hair a little and then splashed my face one more time before setting off down to the bank.

When I walked into the lobby, it was about five before six, so I timed that out right as I had hoped to. There were a few fellows still around but not too many, and I got myself in the line for Mrs. Foss. She saw me and shouted, "Hi, Henry!" which was awful nice and with me not trying to get a check from the stadium into the bank did not make me feel funny for getting a little attention.

After the two boys cleared out in front of me, it was my turn.

"Hello, Mrs. Foss. The usual," I said.

Saying "the usual" right before you are going to ask someone on a date for the first time puts things on a course you have to break out of, but I did not figure this until after I'd said it.

"Right, Henry," she said loudly but without shouting, and she did her figuring out like she always does and started filling in the right forms.

"Mrs. Foss, I was wondering about whether you walk home," I said, trying to sound like it was just a regular thing, but my voice was a little wavy, so it might not have.

Her head popped up.

"Yes, Henry. I could take the trolley I suppose, but it's not too far a walk. I live in the bungalows along Haddaway Road. The new ones," she said, a little proud.

I knew these. They were awfully nice from what I heard, and I figure the company did her a good turn by getting her in there with her husband gone. She had a son, maybe seven years old, who was in with her, from what I understood.

"Well, Mrs. Foss, I could walk you home, if that would help."

She just froze solid for a second, right there in place. It looked a little alarming, I will say.

"Help with what?" she asked, looking at me with squinty eyes like her eyesight was going on her, too. This did not make her more pretty.

There was a fellow behind me in line now, and I would not want to be him listening in on this with it Friday and waiting to cash a check.

"With the walk and all that." I had no idea what to say at this point, which was made clear here.

The fellow behind me let out a groaning noise.

"Thanks, Henry but I know the...." Then she paused and turned real red and looked down. She looked back up and fixed her hair real fast as if doing it quick I might not spot it.

"That would be nice, Henry. Give me five minutes!" she said with a big smile and back to shouting now. She then handed me my $1.50, and I got off that line like a shot.

Once outside I sat down on a little bench in front of the bank. It was a clear night and cool, and I had worked up a little sweat with the asking, too, so I was happy for night air. I will say I picked a good one, and other than having the fellow behind me, I had pulled off my plan like what they would call on the ball field, an old pro. Speaking of that fellow, he came out the door and saw me on the bench.

"Good luck, Rube," was all he said, and then he laughed to himself and kept going. I was set to say something to him as it was an unfriendly laugh, but I was feeling good and not going to let a dope spoil that feeling.

Just a few minutes later Mrs. Foss came out. She smiled as big as ever and walked right up to the bench.

"Well Henry, I'm ready to walk!" she shouted and she looked a little nervous, and this made me feel pretty good. That she could get nervous about a walk with me was a promising start.

If you know the layout of the Point, and since you've gotten this far you know some of it, the town is a little to the northeast of the mill. Looking down at it like a bird might, Haddaway Road is more off to the east, a little in the woods with a creek right behind them. It would be what they call the outskirts of town if the Point was a regular town, but it is not.

We walked away from the bank, and I let Mrs. Foss do the leading as she would know the best way.

"How are things at the bank, Mrs. Foss?"

This was good grounds for a start.

"You can go ahead and call me Colleen, Henry. I'm hardly older than you, I figure. Did you know my name plate at work says 'Mrs. Colleen Foss,' but everybody just skips the Colleen? I'd rather they skip the 'Mrs.' by now." Then she started laughing. This joke would not rate in the top drawer down at the mill, but I pushed out a little laugh back.

"Okay, Colleen, then. How is the bank?"

"It's good, Henry. Most folks seem to put in more than they take out, which is good for us. If it was the other way, we wouldn't be around long. Once in awhile somebody tries to pass me some funny money, but most of it is so bad you really want to laugh. It's hard to make a good fake dollar, you know."

"I will have to try," I said and laughed.

"Just don't hand it to me," she said. "Now that we're not talking official, can I ask you where you get the yellow checks from? I know they're from Baltimore and all, but we're not supposed to be too nosy, so I don't try to figure it out."

I explained about working at the stadium and asked her to keep that to herself, which I thought she would. As I have said she is a real professional at the bank, which was something else I liked about her. You like the person working with all your money being serious about it.

We drifted off onto Sparrows Point Drive, and the town slipped a little ways back from us. There were trees ahead, and if you looked close, you could see the tidiest little houses in there with them, and the lights started popping on when we were walking over, like lightning bugs waking up in the summer, little by little. I never made it down this way much.

"The stadium is just about the nicest place you'd want to see, Colleen. Even if you are not partial to sports, the front gate and the lights and the size of it really make it the tops."

She kept walking and the road got a little rockier as we went along it, so we had to look down more. I noticed now that she wasn't shouting so much as she does at the bank. I wondered why but kept this to myself.

"I'd like to see it, Henry. Maybe when the working is done, you could take me for a trolley car ride up into the city, and we could look at it."

I could feel my pulse up in my neck now, but in a good way. I wasn't expecting this to go so good, and here it was doing just that.

"I could get you there, no trouble at all. I know the ride in like it was nothing," I said.

"I'd like that," she said.

After I got to talking about my work, Colleen— I'll try to call her that now, but it will take some time to get used to it—starting talking about her work. Wilton was killed straight away in July of '18 at Chateau Thierry. She got notice just about ten days later that he was dead. The company was real good to her, and they let her stay on at the mill housing. She said she was broken up, as I could guess, but for her, working was one way to get her mind off Wilton getting killed.

At first she couldn't turn up any work in Sparrows Point, and just up the trolley line in Curtis Creek they were working on some wooden steamers for the war, and for a brief while she got a job up there in an office.

I paused a moment here, because I've heard about those wooden steamers. President Wilson himself ordered a whole lot of them to be built, and fast, so they could get supplies over to Europe quickly, and if they got sunk it was a lot less cost than a regular steamer going down. Thing was, most of them leaked real bad right away and sank like rocks before the Germans had at them. Some of them went straight down into Curtis Creek right after being launched. They are not something people talk much about these days but it was a big deal back then. I'm not sure a single one of them made their way over to the war.

"I have heard about those steamers," I said, leaving out the sinking like rocks part. This made her smile real big, so I am glad I did. After the war there was no need for building leaky steamers, so she ended up down at the bank. She got into Haddaway Road with her boy and folks in '22 right when the houses was first built.

By the time she was done talking, we was at the house. It was fire engine red, and she said that it really was fire engine red, because her father was with the Sparrows Point Fire Department and they'd given him some of the extra paint. It had a screened porch, which was real useful, given the bugs.

"The red's too fancy for me, but it's free paint!" she said, then laughed again.

I started in, too.

"Well Henry, I'm home. Thanks for walking me and thanks for figuring out that I could use the help walking home," she said, a little jumpy.

"It was a treat, and I will take you up on the trip to the stadium someday soon. It will definitely be worth your while," I said.

I stopped and looked at my shoes. I'd not been at this point with a lady since I was a young man, which wasn't the same thing at all.

"Goodnight," she said, and held out her hand to shake.

"Goodnight," I said back. Then a feeling came over me, and I picked up her hand and gave it a quick little kiss. This was probably too much, you are thinking, but the feeling shot in, and it was done. She got all red but was smiling, so I was okay.

"I will see you next Friday, then," I said and then nodded and started backing up. I walked about twenty yards down Haddaway then I turned around. Sure enough she was standing there and waved goodbye to me. That walk home beat Bay Shore Park, it was that good.

CHAPTER 13

Fall in Maryland isn't like it is in Poughkeepsie or even like it is in France, now that I've been talking about that lately. In Maryland fall pulls up a chair before winter and takes its time, and sometimes you wonder about winter and if it's coming at all.

Although I was not enjoying the notion of being singled out at the football game, the change in weather for the better certainly made life on the line at the mill a little easier and being out of doors at the stadium all that much more pleasant.

In early fall most every year that I can remember, the rain dries up a bit around Baltimore, and the ground gets baked, and everything turns brown for awhile. It was like this up at the stadium, and the slopes that I tended with Mr. Spector began to break up and crater quite a bit. When I say crater, I mean the ground was so dry and hard that the rain would wash down it when it came and make a ditch or gully that would just take everything down with it.

By October some rain set in, and it helped when it came to patching up the late summer damage. Mr. Spector has been here a couple falls now, and he has some good ideas on how to fix the general mess that the dry weather made, so we moved along well enough.

As far as being part of the halftime show at the game, there wasn't too much talk of that, but Overman, when I saw him, made it clear that we were still on. We didn't have another one of our talking-about-the-bleachers-but-not-talking-about-the-bleachers conversations, and for that I was glad. I found my old uniform tucked away on mothballs in the back of my closet at the house and tried it on. It still fit and with the way I'd been working every day it was not surprising that I had not put on any extra weight for being a laggard.

I should talk a little about Duncan and Carr. I did not know Carr but just a little, him being a sergeant in the battalion and me spending more time with the other privates. He also did not train at Upton but instead was one of the western boys who joined us very late, right before we got into the fight.

Duncan I did know, and I knew well the things that he'd seen. Getting back to the States and getting all that he saw out of his thoughts would take some time if it was ever to happen. In the Argonne, Duncan was on the left flank of what you have surely heard in the papers as called the Pocket. The Pocket was shaped like a flattened football, and it ran along the side of a hill. The Germans came at the left hard because the other sides were tougher to approach. Duncan was out there with a machine gun crew.

You would think being attached to a machine gun crew would be a good thing in a fight, but it is certainly not. Everyone is trying to kill you in particular because they know if you are done for everything is going to get a lot easier for them. Me, I was just a soldier and not a machine gunner, so the Germans didn't have any special desire to have me dead other than they were generally trying to kill all of us.

With Duncan on a gun, and living through it, he'd seen several other crews lost to the Germans. Let me point out that losing a crew means a lot more than it sounds like. Guys get blown up right next to you or bayoneted and run through with a knife or they are gassed or even at the end the Germans tried to light us on fire with these terrible torch guns that I can barely think about let alone describe.

One night in the Pocket—we were surrounded for five nights—I came in behind Duncan's machine gun crew with two other privates, Wilson and Corelli, to help see them through to morning. Here we were, crouched in the little nest they'd scraped out to protect our flank. An Italian boy named Catino, who didn't know a lick of English, was sitting there dead and stiff, part of his face shot through.

Next to him was a fellow named Flanagan, his arm all torn up and wrapped in old bandages that looked like they may have come from Catino. We ran out of bandages in the Pocket early, so we had to scrounge regular.

Duncan was crouched behind the gun, with Flanagan no use and Catino dead but nowhere to take him. The boys started right in and moved Catino's body off to the side and propped up Flanagan against him while I unwrapped some hard bread and a canteen of water that I'd carried in a sack swung over my shoulder. Part of the problem with the Pocket, and there was a lot, was having no food. Corelli knew Flanagan, both from the Bowery, and was bucking him up and raising a canteen up to his mouth.

"Tastes better than back home, Corelli," I heard Flanagan say between drinks.

"We'll be back drinking some of that dirty water soon enough," Corelli said.

"Duncan, how is it here?" I asked.

He jumped like I woke him up, but he was not asleep.

"They are coming through now."

"Where are they?"

"They're to our right. Flanagan's gone out after them and not come back since yesterday. I don't want to lay into them because he might still be over that way."

Wilson and Corelli stopped for an instant and looked at me. Flanagan was too busy drinking and eating what he could to care much about what Duncan was saying, or if it made sense. He didn't even look up.

"Duncan, Flanagan's back. If the Jerries start in, let into them. I'll try to cover you to this side."

Just as I said that, I heard a familiar screaming whistle from above.

"Down!" I shouted.

A mortar shell blew to our right. Wilson and Corelli were down near me, but Duncan stayed at the gun. When the smoke cleared, we lifted our heads. Duncan, I could see, was okay.

"Anyone hit?"

"I'm okay, Dawson," said Corelli.

"I'm alright, Private," said Wilson.

I was relieved for a moment, and then I saw Flanagan. He was not down low enough and his upper half was all blown apart, mostly gone. It is too horrible to say more than that. Corelli started to cry. Duncan started firing and Wilson pressed back against the wall of the nest with all his might like he could get out straight through the dirt.

Those boys was in this spot for five straight days and through the nights, which were more terrible. No one should ever be in such a place, not for a single night.

I was surprised to see Duncan on the list of fellows coming to Venable. When we split up after the war he wasn't presentable and battle exhaustion as they called it had overtaken him. This made sense given what he'd seen, but people did not make allowance for these horrible things. You were home, the war was over, and we'd won. All was regular again.

* * *

It finally came together in early November that I was to meet Carr and Duncan and we was to prepare for the ceremony. It was a Sunday and Overman called me into his office just as I was walking up towards the Administration Building from the trolley on 33rd.

"Dawson!" he shouted and then waved me towards him.

Instead of walking into his office, we walked straight on through the building and out onto the playing field. This was the first time I got a view of the stadium from this point, and it was a sight. The grass was in perfect shape, and around the far end almost all of the extra seating that had taken so much work was in place. There were little crowds of people moving around and finding their way to their seats. You couldn't help feeling more than a little pride looking around and thinking you had a hand in making this place what it was.

"No game today is there, Mr. Overman?" I asked.

He looked up at the crowds of people.

"No, the ushers are rehearsing for the big game plus we're showing off our progress to a few important people without a big crowd in here."

If he was agitated from our last conversation in his office, he did not show it.

"Carr and Duncan are coming along here any moment. That Duncan's a funny fellow, isn't he?" he asked.

I bit my tongue, as they say, because Duncan wasn't funny at all. He was all wore through in a way that Overman would never know. Whoever thought it was a good idea to trot him out for this was the one I'd call funny.

While I was thinking that, nothing came out of my mouth, so Overman just kept going on from where he'd left off.

"We're going to do a rehearsal ourselves to make sure we get all of you to the right spot on the day of the game. I know you work Saturdays at your regular job, so they are coming today."

He paused, maybe waiting for me to thank him, I don't know. If I never did hear another word about the Argonne, I would die a happy man.

"Yes, sir," was all I said.

As I was talking to Overman, I saw the doorway that we'd just come through over his shoulder, and out from back of the Administration Building came old Duncan and Carr. Carr strode out regular as anything, and behind him was Duncan. He shuffled out, like someone was pushing him from the back.

They both looked around the field, it was too hard to resist taking it in. The sun was still moving up on our right, and it was lighting up the stadium more and more with each minute. The shadow was gradually rolling back from the grass.

Duncan saw me and ran over. The Army sent most of the 308th packing in 1919, and I'd not seen him since then. That puts us five years out, which is hard to imagine.

"Henry!" he said when he'd gotten up close.

We shook like the pals we had once been. If you have not seen him, Duncan is over six feet, a tall fellow, and he has wavy brown hair that looks all coiled up in the middle and kind of wiry with parts of his forehead showing pretty clearly. He is skinny, real skinny, and you got the feeling in the service that he could go without food a long while because he didn't need any to stay that thin.

"Well, well, if it isn't Frank Duncan. How are you?"

He did not answer right away, like it took some thinking.

"I'm good, Henry. I'm working on the docks down here, and somebody figured out I was with the 308th. Don't know how, but I figure it's good for a free meal maybe."

Then he laughed his kind of shaky laugh, and as I looked him over, it was still old torn up Duncan, but he seemed a little better than when I last saw him. I have found that getting out of a war generally has a beneficial effect on a person.

I then walked over to Carr.

"Private Henry Dawson, Sergeant," I said, offering my hand.

He shook it a little stiffly. Carr looked older, his belly bigger and his face fatter, but not in a jolly sort of way, more like his face was pumped up with water. He was about my height, 5'9" or so, and a lot thicker. His hair was jet black and he looked like he hadn't shaved in awhile. He had the same dark shadows under his eyes that many of us took on in the Pocket from want of food and sleep.

"This all your idea, Dawson?" he said without a hint of what I would call friendliness.

"No, Sergeant. They was going to build this place without even asking me," I said with a laugh. You joke around the boys even if you haven't seen them in awhile. It got us through some long nights over there, being funny.

Duncan laughed beside me, and this did not sit well with Sergeant Carr—now just Norman.

"What next?" Carr said, turning to Overman.

Overman clapped his hands together like we were starting in on a big adventure and he was in charge and about to get us moving.

"Okay then boys, we're going to pull this together at halftime of the big game. I can guess who you'll be rooting for."

Carr just stared at him, and then Duncan shouted "Army!" back at Overman, loudly enough that Hadley looked embarrassed. Several people in the stands turned and looked down our way.

"Right. Now the players will head this way at the break for the half."

He then walked us over to one of the side arches that led into the locker room. Overman did a lot of pointing and asking if we understood. I think he was fancying himself a colonel at this particular moment.

"Do we get fed?" asked Carr.

"What was that, Sergeant?" Overman asked.

"Chow. Do we get food? From what I understand there's a meal involved, right boys?"

He then turned to us with his eyebrows lifted.

"Yes," said Duncan.

I didn't say anything. I didn't care much for Overman, and I liked Carr less with every word and wasn't going to weigh in on his account.

"Well, yes," said Overman. "That and the battle medals from the mayor himself."

"I'll take the grub first," Carr replied, turning away. He pulled out a pack of cigarettes, struck up a match, and took a long draw on one.

Overman turned to me next, clearly disappointed that a man could think about food before a medal. Colonel Overman's troops weren't showing what the Frogs called *Esprit de Corps*.

Out of the corner of my eye I spotted Duncan. His right hand began going in and out of his coat pocket, slowly first, then picking up speed a little as nobody said anything. His left hand began loosening his collar at the same time.

"Yes, Mr. Overman, that will be a pleasure," I said, with more excitement in my voice than I was feeling.

Then our little gathering just sort of broke up. Carr walked away towards the Administration Building. Overman followed him and then it was just me and Duncan standing there.

"That it, Henry?" he asked, watching Hadley and Carr walk away. His hand started working the pocket again. Looking closer, I could see now clear enough that it was threadbare.

"That's it, Duncan. You get yourself up here an hour before the game. I'll meet you right at that bench over there."

I pointed to a bench tucked up against the wall in the archway. I hoped it would be there come game time.

"Sure, right at that spot. An hour before the game sharp. I'll get the game time in the *Sun* the day before," Duncan said.

"Thinking on your feet, as always," I said.

Then I gave him a big smile and patted his shoulder, pressing in to try to push some steadiness back in. You do that.

"I'll talk to Overman about the chow, but get yourself breakfast. I'll be in my uniform and will look for you. Just like old times."

He smiled. We was all there together, me, Duncan, and even Carr. Duncan and me had trained out at Camp Upton on the Island, and although that was either a buggy, miserable place or a freezing cold, miserable place that first year, there was no killing, and we were in it together. Part of the reason

I took up life at the Point so easy was that it was better than Camp Upton and of course a lot better than France with us mostly living on the ground over there and being shot at. There was no Porter back at Upton, only a sergeant, and he was always mad at you or screaming something. It seemed like half the boys at camp couldn't even speak English when we first got there. But that only made him shout all the louder.

CHAPTER 14

That night I could find no rest in bed. Seeing Carr and Duncan got me thinking. I thought a lot about Camp Upton and how they first came in from around the city, and then later they added some boys like me from upstate and New England, and finally some boys joined the 308th from out west.

Duncan was one of the boys from upstate but got there after me. He only had about a month at Upton before we shoved off. For a long time at camp we had no guns so we practiced with fake ones, and believe that or not, it is true. They finally got us Springfields, and we felt a little more like soldiers. How Duncan ended up with a machine gun, I do not know for certain, but I can guess it was because a machine gunner was taken out before him.

The last group from the West came in right before we headed over, and they only had maybe a week with the Springfields. Once we were over in France with the whole 77th division, nobody in headquarters paid much attention to who were the new boys and who were there from the start, and they just threw us out there together like we'd all been trained equal.

That was a horrible turn for some of the western boys.

At first we fought with the Tommies, and they were all spit and polish, at least the officers, and we didn't really blend like they had hoped. Then Pershing got us out from under them, and we eventually ended up with the French boys. They were all worn out and weren't much for the spit and polish and all, and in that way I think we matched up with them a little better, but they were all fought thin and they didn't mind an American getting to a fight before they did, if you know what I mean. They had ways of finding things that slowed them down. Nobody said it, but you could see it plain as day after awhile.

Here's where I first got to know Duncan a little better than your average fellow at Upton. We were billeted in an old barn in France on one of our first nights over there, before we really knew what a mess things would be. It's funny, we thought coming over there that we'd be sleeping in chateaus and drinking wine and such, which is just plain stupid, but you get ideas like that, not knowing any better.

Duncan and I shared a burned out farm with a couple pigs and four other privates. He started out a real calm sort of guy, and he fell asleep next to a pig like he'd been doing it all his life, although he was from Buffalo and not a farm boy at all.

"This pig'll do just fine as long as he lies still, Dawson," he said with a big booming laugh, the kind that made you feel good just to have heard it. He patted me on the knee, said "Good night," pulled his helmet down over his eyes, and was asleep in no time while me and the other privates fidgeted around all night trying to find a level spot on the floor of that barn. It was quieter there than it has ever been. You look at those nights awfully fondly, too, same as Upton. We were together and there was no killing, and even if you were scared that there would be, you just hadn't seen it.

* * *

I took to wearing gloves now for the outdoor work at Venable. The change was on, with the stadium getting colder and the heat at the Point making it a better place to work indoors as we moved towards winter.

The week before the game, we did some finish up work. They'd put some seats everywhere they could fit them, and some of the last spots were right in front of the concrete wall at the base of the stands. They planned on sitting some of the cadets and middies down there, hopefully not so close that they'd mix it up.

Mr. Spector and me got pulled off from our hill work and assigned to working on those last seats. I liked this just fine, especially since the stadium was pretty much polished off and it was a beauty to behold, if I do say so.

We'd got the cinders on the track down just right, and it was a perfect spot for some of the parading that was due up for the game. Right above the field in the first rows of the bleachers was this little boxed-in concrete area where, if you can believe it, the President of the United States was going to sit. Today Mr. Spector and me was putting the final seats down right in front of this very box.

"You nail straight now, Henry. You good with that shovel, but I've seen your hammering, and it is not especially mentionable," said Mr. Spector.

"If the President's taking a close look at the nails around the place, we're in trouble."

I may have been the only fellow in the whole stadium who could claim to have a hand in both making the nails and hammering them in on this day. They came in barrels from the Point, and if you'd seen the giant room we stored them in down at the mill, you'd have not thought it possible that the world could use so many.

I told Mr. Spector as much, and he looked at a nail in his hand and then gave it a kiss and tucked it in his chest pocket.

"I thought these nails were too nice for hammering away," he said, laughing.

And so that afternoon went, with me and Mr. Spector finishing off the hammering. It was a chilly day—I'd put it in the 40's—when we personally finished the last stands in the entire place. There was some painting of the section numbers still to be done, but that was just the icing, not the cake.

It was an hour before quitting time, and we shook hands like those fellows did when they completed the railway all the way across the country. Mr. Spector struck a pose like the camera was there, which is about as showy as he gets.

"Okay then, we're ready for 80,000 in here," he said.

With that done we grabbed his tools and got ready for our walk to the top. Word was that folks who worked at the stadium could buy tickets for the game at a special lowered price. I figured I was going to be given a ticket for the halftime part. Mr. Spector said that he was not getting any unless they were free. I understand there was to be a colored section for the game, so I thought maybe him and Reginald might want to pick up some tickets.

"Lower is not free," is all Mr. Spector said to that.

"I'd still like to head over and see what's going on at the ticket booth. I'd like to see how much lower they are."

"You thinking of buying one for you and all your lady friends you saving up to ask?" he said. I did not especially appreciate this, it being sarcastic as it was.

"No, just one. She works at a bank, though, so she probably won't need them tickets to be any lower," I said, showing off a little. I do not figure they give people at the bank some of the extra money to take home with them like they do with the old bread at a bakery, but I let out with that anyways.

"Well, Henry, you have finally heard something I've been saying. Sure, let's get on over there and take a look at what they have."

CHAPTER 15

We worked our way up through the bleachers, passing the little concrete area, and I must say I spent a minute sitting in the very spot that I do believe the President will be in.

Almost straight up from the President's box was the bleachers that had been added. In front of them was the walkway that could take you all the way around the stadium, and the back half jutted in behind the upper bleachers. This was the path that would take you over to the tool shed. We got up to it quickly enough. We walked together under the bleachers and it turned awfully cold awfully fast. Mr. Spector shivered and then said, "Let's get on through here."

Much of the crew now had gone as it was late in the afternoon and the stadium was nearly completed to boot. Those that were still working were gone over to the ticket booth, and down on the field I could hear none other than Overman himself shouting through a bullhorn. He was standing in the back of a flatbed truck that was driving on the gravel track we put down that was not for trucks.

"If you head over to the ticket booths now, gentlemen, you will enjoy special prices as a thank you for all your hard work."

That sounded nice enough, even coming from Overman, and I continued on towards the tool shed with Mr. Spector. It was darker under the seats, as you would expect.

There were two men in the shadows, and I couldn't make them out very well. They were tucked in under the bleachers tight to my left, and they were just sitting there, not going anywhere or doing anything, sitting so still you almost didn't know they were there. I took a quick look over, and Mr. Spector, who does not miss a trick, saw me.

"Keep walking, Henry," he whispered under his breath, keeping his head looking forward the whole time.

We kept going and before long, we were putting the tools away. While we were doing this, Mr. Spector began in.

"They're keeping me on here, Henry. After the game and all. Said this place will need a few hands even in winter with the big ballgame done for the year. Mr. Overman told me this week. I've been worrying sick about it every week as this game's been getting closer."

Funny thing was, with my job at the mill, I hadn't given much thought as to what I'd be doing after the game.

"Mr. Overman said I can keep you on some Sundays if you want. You got a feel for the place that's coming along pretty good, and I figure it would help us both out if you stuck around. Plus in the winter you don't have to work every Sunday, so maybe you can get out and take that girl to see the windows over at Hutzler's around Christmas."

I can't set down how his words made me feel. I knew I kept up at the mill, and I knew the coal was coming on that belt and that was that, no matter if I was there or not. But having somebody ask you to stick around because of what you did in particular—well that felt pretty good.

"Sure, Mr. Spector, that would work fine. Thank you."

Then I shook his hand, and we sealed it.

"We got a deal then," he said.

With that he closed up the little tool shed, and we began walking back out from under the bleachers. It was pretty dark now under those seats, and as I should have expected, given that his sight is as old as his body, Mr. Spector caught his boot on a little board that was lying there. They were everywhere, covering the ground like fallen leaves. He went down, hard.

He came up slowly, holding his right hand. It was cut right across the palm, the blood slowly coloring the sawdust that now covered it.

"You alright, Mr. Spector?"

"I'm fine. My eyes ain't fine, but I'm fine."

He wiped his hand off with his rag and then wrapped it round, holding it with his good hand as we walked.

We kept moving through the bleachers, and once again I could sense boys underneath, but I could not make them out so well. Truth was, half the people I knew thought Prohibition was wrong, not the drinking, and wouldn't have minded the liquor under the stands, not one bit. It still didn't sit well with me, but I kept moving.

Mr. Spector seemed none the worse for wear now that his hand was wrapped up. He followed me around to the steps leading down the slope to the ticket booth.

"Well, Henry, you set?"

"I am. If you're hand is alright, let's go see what deals Overman's got for us."

CHAPTER 16

To explain what happened next at the stadium, I need to first take a minute to describe the place itself. It is a bowl with the Administration Building and gate out front at one end and the bowl making its way around the rest of the stadium. It's almost like a big letter D from the sky with the Administration Building being the flat part of the D and the curved part being the bowl. There were steps coming down the sides of the stadium in a few spots, and connecting the sets of steps about halfway down the hill were some side stairs that went over to the bathrooms. You could get to the bathrooms either going up or down. They were pushed directly into the side of the hill.

If you can picture that, it will help. I would regularly make trips there, as you might guess, during the course of a day. Mr. Spector said he wanted to stop by the bathroom to get some of the dirt out of his cut, so I told him I'd walk down to the bottom of the hill and he could meet me there.

I walked down and then sat on the bottom step for about ten minutes. Now older folks don't move all that fast, but this was still longer than what you might expect. It was getting colder too, and I had sat long enough, so I turned and walked back up to the bathrooms.

When I finally made it up there, I opened the bathroom door, and the smell from too many folks using the place shot out at me. It wasn't enough to knock you over, but it could push you backwards some. It was that bad. In the midsummer it was worse.

"Mr. Spector?" I shouted. It was mostly dark in there, and the lights weren't on yet.

My voice echoed back to me. No answer.

I pressed the light switch next to the door and then flipped through all the doors on the bathroom stalls and did not find him. I quickly had enough of that stink and got out of there. I then looked down the hill to my left and right and saw the usual business going on and some boys now gathered around the ticket booth.

"Damn mess they're making!"

I heard Mr. Spector say from somewhere nearby, but his words was muffled.

"Mr. Spector?" I shouted again.

I got no answer. Then from behind the bathroom, which was built too far into the hill to seem like it could have anything behind it, out comes Mr. Spector. He was filthy, dirtier than we got on any regular day.

"What were you doing back there? How did you get behind the bathrooms?"

He dusted himself off, which did little good.

"Oh you can get back there, 'specially if you a fool and have a shovel and some liquor to hide."

I wondered what the hell he was talking about. I walked to the side he'd just come from and saw a board thrown off and lying against the hill, out of place. Then, right behind the back wall of the poured cement bathroom was a hole about chest high that looked like it was big enough to fit a man into. I bent down and stuck my head in a little ways.

It took a minute for my eyes to adjust to the darkness.

Well, goddamn. It was a little cave somebody dug, with wooden supports holding up the left side and the back of the bathroom as the right side. Somebody had even put in what looked like rough wooden beams to support the dirt ceiling. It was about six feet into it and maybe three or four feet wide. If this didn't look like a dugout from the war, nothing did. An old doughboy made this.

Along the dirt wall, from floor to top, were stacked wooden cases. I didn't have to guess what they were. A couple of bottles were broken on the floor and stunk of dirt and whiskey.

"This something?" Mr. Spector said and spit.

"How'd you find it?"

Mr. Spector kept looking around like he'd lost something, growing more agitated every second.

"I look at this hill every time I go anywhere. I don't know how long it's been here, but it ain't been too long. Otherwise I'd have seen it before. That board was covering it up, and unless you like me and are looking for problems with the dirt around here, it was doing a good enough job for most folks."

We were both in there now. Mr. Spector was pressing on the dirt wall to our left, as if it'd tell him how it got there if he pressed into it. I have never seen him so troubled.

"I spend two years making this place presentable, get it nearly done, and then somebody comes and does this. Next big rain this thing's collapsing like paper and this liquor here's gonna be under three feet of mud. The whole hill's going to pile up behind this wall. They can't figure that out?" He stepped back and looked down at the boxes.

"It ain't right. Have your booze if you will, but don't ruin this place on account of you too stupid to find a place to hide it."

If this reminds you of my talking with Overman, that is no surprise.

"You're right. Now let's get out of here. I'll let Overman know. I think he knows there's booze around but I don't think he knows they're tearing this place up like this."

We both started working our way out of the dugout when I saw a shadow in the opening. What sun that was left was coming in behind whoever it was, so I could not make him out. He started in and I was the closest to the opening, so he bumped right into me. I stumbled back, knocking Mr. Spector down.

"You alright, Mr. Spector?" I said and reached down for him.

"What the hell are you doing in here, Spector?" the voice shouted.

Mr. Spector was up like a man half his age after hearing his name called out.

"I don't know who you are, but what the hell is this? You ruining this place. You don't have enough common sense to put this stuff in your basement and not ruin the stadium digging holes behind a goddamn bathroom?" Mr. Spector shouted right back at him.

The man was coming into focus. I didn't know him. It wasn't Russell and I could not place him. He had arms like tree trunks and nearly blocked out the light behind him.

His voice got quieter, but you could tell he was forcing it quiet.

"Listen you old fool. Get the hell out of here right now and shut your mouth about this. It don't concern you. Get out and I might leave you be."

"We'll see if it concerns Mr. Overman," Mr. Spector let out.

I squeezed Mr. Spector's arm, hard. He was just seeing red and not thinking.

"You mention this to Overman, Spector, and it will be the last thing you mention to anyone."

That was about enough for me, too, and I ran forward and sent a hard shoulder into the thug's belly, knocking him to the side of the opening and turning to grab Mr. Spector's arm to get him the hell out of there. The thug let it stand, as I might have knocked some wind out of him. I didn't wait to find out. Once we were passed, he immediately pressed further into the little dugout and was lost to sight.

"You alright?" I said when we got through.

"I am. They're spoiling all our damn work, Henry. You were right. They can't do that. Not after all this."

That was right, of course, but we needed to stop reacting for a minute and start thinking.

"Alright, then. We'll take it on tomorrow. Let's just leave it be for a minute until we figure something to do. That fellow's too worried about his liquor right now to come bother with us. Let's get down and away from here to see about those tickets."

As you can guess, that incident left a lot hanging in the air. The fellow knew Mr. Spector's name now, which wasn't good. I didn't know him, and I'm not sure he made me out, so I didn't have a lot to worry about right away in the way of trouble, but with Mr. Spector, I could not be sure. A Negro telling a fellow, who was up to no good for starters, that he's stupid isn't going to sit well with him. He also knew that Mr. Spector was going to talk to Overman. This was more trouble.

We made our way down to the bottom of the hill again like we planned to, but it wasn't right anymore. I wanted to buy a ticket but couldn't that minute, I was still so riled.

"Let's head out. This can wait," I said.

"No, Henry. You got a lady friend now, so you go get her a ticket. Don't let him spoil it. I'm settled down some. Least you have coming is a ticket and a nice time with a lady for all this work you done plus the trouble of putting a good shoulder to a guy," Mr. Spector said.

He let go a little smile out the side of his mouth. This made me want to laugh, but I couldn't. I went ahead and bought a ticket for Mrs. Foss for what was a square deal.

I usually catch the trolley right there out in front of the stadium, but I knew another spot a couple blocks south where I could meet up with the next car heading crosstown to the 26. It was a Sunday, and they didn't run too steady, so it gave me time in between cars to walk a bit if I missed the first.

Instead of walking towards the front gate like we always did, Mr. Spector turned around and started heading back in the opposite direction to the far side of the stadium.

"You're not heading back to that dugout now, are you?" I asked him.

"No, no. When you stay this late they already closed up the front of the stadium because it's a big production, and they need to get going with it about a half hour before they shut down. They send us round back to 36th where we can get out."

So we walked around the foot of the stadium, back away from the Administration Building and towards 36th Street.

"I'm catching the trolley down at 29th and Greenmount," I said. He knew this wasn't my usual spot.

"Henry, I know what you're thinking. They won't trouble with me. Don't worry. Mr. Overman ain't perfect, but he won't let them have at me."

If he had faith in Overman to protect him, I knew all the more that I should skip that first car. Overman wasn't here, didn't mind the liquor, and seemed to me no great friend of Harold Spector when I last talked to him. Plus if it ever came to defending someone in a scrape, Overman would be as helpful as a sack of potatoes. That was clear enough after taking one look at him.

So we kept walking.   North Baltimore in November on a Sunday night is a quiet place, and you can forget you are in a city easy enough. On the far end of the stadium, things aren't all built up yet, and the birds were making a racket as they settled down for the night. It was not like walking down Pratt Street with the ships coming in at all hours and always folks around. It's still a remote place, even in the city.

We walked back along Ednor Road towards the front.   The stadium's big slope was up above our right shoulders. Venable looked like a mountain as it got darker. After a time, we got to the front of the Administration Building. The building rose high above us, and the columns looked like they almost glowed in the bluish light. This is no exaggeration. They had a couple lamps on in the far corners of the front wings of the entrance, and they threw some light, but not much. There was nobody round us, nobody at all.

Mr. Spector stopped in front of one of the columns and turned to look at me.

"Them bootleggers are digging their hole in this," he said. Then with two fingers on his left hand he tapped on one of the columns. "We're just a short spell away from being set here Henry, they can't ruin that on us. They can't."

We'd both had thrown a lot into building up Venable. I'd seen places called woods that didn't have a tree in them and were sickly and full of swarms of flies and miserable as far as you could see. Bit by bit they'd turned from forests into places you could not imagine a seed could have ever set its roots down. Here they'd done something different altogether, taking the mess that was once Venable Park and building something that people could come to even if there was no game and they just wanted to set back and take the view from the top. And now they were rifling through the middle of it.

CHAPTER 17

As we were passing the last column on the far left, I saw a shadow move under the light thrown by one of the lamps. I wasn't sure if Mr. Spector had seen it, but now I saw it again just a second later. It was staying back a ways but sticking with us. I looked out the corner of my eye a third time. It was two shadows. I didn't say anything at first, not wanting to alarm him over nothing, if it was nothing. We kept walking and making our way out to 33rd, which felt like it pushed back 100 yards from where I last saw it. My stomach sank as I could still see a little group moving along with us. They weren't hiding so much anymore and they were moving with a purpose. The light thrown off the stadium caught them full from behind and they were now a single shadow making quick progress in our direction. There was no mistaking that they were approaching us.

"Mr. Spector, we've got a few fellows walking with us along the wall over there. They might just be walking, but I'm letting you know."

We got out towards the road. The group was away from the stadium light so a little harder to make out, but from what I could tell it was even bigger than just a moment ago. Thirty-third stretched out in front of us. I usually never walked this leg, and it was going slow, too slow. Mr. Spector did not walk at a fast pace once he left the stadium, and he certainly was not now.

The road was cobbled and dirty, and I heard a baby crying from a nearby apartment, and then I heard footsteps scuffing on the cinders and cobblestones behind us. I got pretty good at listening for Germans in the war and being real quiet and figuring out their numbers. This was something you had to do over there to stay alive, and now here I was doing it back home. There were four or maybe five of them.

They were closing, and we were not going to open up any space on them at this pace. We were heading into a dark stretch where 33rd dips down and trees stretch across from both sides of the street, darkening it like a tunnel. It was time to stop.

"Mr. Spector, they're going to catch up with us. You keep walking, and I'll stop here. I don't think they'll mean real trouble. If I settle them down, they will leave me be and you can be home."

"I appreciate that Henry, but I'm not abiding it. Let's turn around if we got to."

I slowed up and turned to face the group, hoping that they'd be gone but knowing they would not. I took a step out ahead of Mr. Spector, a little closer to the group. He stepped right up next to me.

"Alright boys, you caught up to us," I shouted to them. "Say whatever it is you followed us out here to say, and then we'll be done."

I didn't think they were out here for talking. At first no one said anything in return. My hope was that we'd startled them by stopping instead of just trying to beat a path away.

"Dawson," said a fellow. It was Russell. "We didn't look for any trouble, but the two of you both came looking for it. Why you're wasting your time over some liquor, I have no idea. Nobody gives a damn about it being there but you."

I looked at him. He was bigger than me and broad, with a neck that didn't come out of his collar as far as it might and a beard that ran down it into his shirt. There was three fellows to his left and one short solid guy to his right. He was the one I'd put my shoulder into earlier at the dugout. If there were not five of them, he would be getting the same shoulder.

"We've stopped thinking about the liquor, Russell. We're just going home, same as you should," I said.

"What about you, Spector? You stopped thinking about it or are you letting on to Overman tomorrow? If you think he'll step in, you are out of your thick head, and we will stove it in if you can't figure that out."

Russell turned to face Mr. Spector now. Mr. Spector looked at the ground and started scuffing the toe of his boot against some of the cobblestones, slowly at first then a little faster. I know he wanted to fire back and it was taking everything he had in him not too.

Russell waited and nothing came out of Mr. Spector.

"He forgot about it, Russell. Leave it be," I said.

Nothing, coming from a Negro, was too much for a guy like Russell. He didn't care what I said, he just kept looking at Mr. Spector. He had four thugs with him and an old man, colored at that, not giving him what he wanted to hear was more than he could take. He started walking towards us and the group moved in at his side.

"Slow down, Russell," I said.

"Dawson, I gave you a chance there, but the old fool doesn't have enough sense to take it," he said.

The five moved closer to me, and I could see Mr. Spector out the corner of my eye. I moved in front to block their path to him. As I did, two men were on me. I got into the first one good with my right shoulder, tackling him and he was down, but two others were then on my back and I had an arm around my neck. I caught a blow to the cheek and felt a tooth loosen, and I threw a wild left back over my head and heard a crack that was not my hand. A weight came off my back and the arm loosened from my neck.

For a moment I could see Mr. Spector stepping in towards me but the other two quickly took him to the ground. I pushed towards them with everything I had, but an instant later my arms were pinned and my chin down on the street, cutting open as it hit. Mr. Spector was going down beneath two men in front of me and I saw one rear back with a brick and I prayed that it was for me. It came down with a sickening thud and Mr. Spector was faced down on the street next to my head. I broke free again and was up on my elbows and got myself over his head to keep them back. A blow to the back of my head followed and then all was lost to me.

CHAPTER 18

I woke up with a throbbing that I have never known. The room shook each time I breathed, moving away as I drew in and flying back towards me as I let go. I started to get dizzy but shut my eyes to fend it off. I took my left hand, I could not move my right, and lifted it to my face to steady things. I had a bandage across my nose, and it was puffy around my right eye, which I could only open with some trouble. I was missing part of one upper tooth on the right side, and it was sharp enough to cut my tongue. My chin was stitched sideways right at the point. It felt rough as a cord of rope when I touched it.

My right hand was all bound up and held in place just above my bed by a pulley. The rest of me, just by looking, was okay. A curtain surrounded me on three sides with a wall to my left. I was in a hospital. Out a window you could see lights on buildings but I did not know what time of day it was.

"Mr. Dawson?" a woman's voice said, from my right. It was a nurse. She must have been sitting there the whole time. It hurt to turn my head.

"Yes, ma'am."

"How do you feel?"

"Worse than hell. Where am I?" I asked

"You're at Marine Hospital," she answered.

"How's Mr. Spector?

"Is that the colored gentleman?"

"Yes."

"We'll have to see. He's still not come to. The doctors are tending to him as best they can. He's badly hurt."

"Did somebody arrest the fellows who hit him?"

"Well, if you mean the men that you were in the exchange with, one's in the hospital as well. I don't know about the others."

"Is he dead?"

There was silence then some rustling before she cleared her throat like people do when there's nothing in there.

"No, the dead are in the morgue, Mr. Dawson. He's injured."

"Are any of them in the morgue?" I asked.

She moved closer to me so I could see her. She pursed her lips like a teacher and glared. I did not give one damn.

"No."

The talking was taxing my head so I leaned back and closed my eyes.

"You need to rest. You can leave tomorrow afternoon. You have a broken finger and some facial injuries, but fortunately you'll be fine," she said.

* * *

When I next awoke, the sun was coming up and shining brightly through my window which was not easy on my head. The room was chilly like a big building is in the morning. My curtain was still closed but I could hear people walking across the tile floor, echoing each time they stepped. This did not help my head, either.

The curtain was still drawn around my bed and I couldn't see out other than through the window. I wanted to look in on Mr. Spector. In the war, I was in the hospital one time for a short spell after breathing in some gas and if you groaned loud enough or shouted for an orderly, then somebody came pretty quick if there wasn't too many boys to handle.

I tried saying "nurse" out loud to see what would happen. I heard a pair of shoes click to a stop not too far away, and then they kept going, so I said "nurse" a little louder now, and they clicked again and moved this way, stopping outside my curtain.

"Dawson," I said.

The curtain pulled back a little, and a nurse stuck her head in.

"Mr. Dawson, you need to be a little more quiet. A lot of men are still sleeping."

"Yes ma'am. I was just trying to get your attention."

"Okay, you have it. What was it that you needed?" she said.

"Well, first I really need to make a visit to the bathroom," I said.

"If you can get out of bed, it's right across the hall. I'll help you. If not, there's a pan next to your bed on the night table."

"Thank you. There's a patient here named Mr. Harold Spector. He's colored. I would like to visit him."

She looked at me, worried.

"Well, he's not on this floor, he's in the colored ward. I can have someone take you to see him before you leave us. I see on our charts that you're leaving today."

She kept flipping through some papers and then said, "Your right ring finger is broken. With the cast you should be fine in about six weeks. Come back to us then, and we'll take it off. A doctor will explain everything before you leave. How do you feel now?"

"Better than yesterday, if it was yesterday."

She softened up a little with this and rested her hand on my head like she was feeling for a temperature. She had an Irish face, with a thin nose and round cheeks that did not hang too low and her hair was as red as fire. She still looked worried, but pushed out a smile through it like a nurse will.

"Try to get some rest, it's still early and you can stay into the afternoon. I'll have another nurse look in on you in an hour," she said then nodded and turned away, pulling back the curtain and leaving me on my own. Off her heels went echoing down to the far end of the hall. I was in a hospital gown, and my clothes were folded and sitting on the radiator under the window.

Later I got dressed, which took some work, and I hurt all over. After I was in my clothes, a doctor stopped by with a different nurse and told me how to take care of my finger and when to come back to take off the cast. He was a short, pudgy man and was sweating badly when he came in, like he'd run a mile to get here.

He explained a few more things, then threw in, "Don't try to punch anybody again until it comes off." He said this plainly.

"If that anybody doesn't come at me and an old man, I surely won't."

He frowned, which was fine with me. After they left, an orderly took me to the colored ward. It was a floor just like mine but in a faraway section of the hospital. He led me to Mr. Spector's bed.

Mr. Spector looked terrible. His eyes were mostly closed. They would open just a tiny bit, and then they'd press more tightly closed. His head was bandaged and his right hand all wrapped up. At his side was Reginald, stooped down in the chair, staring at the floor and not picking his head up when I came in.

"Reginald, I'm sorry about your father."

He didn't look up.

"Do you know how he's doing?" I asked.

"His head's wrapped up, and he's out cold in a hospital bed. Why'd they do this to him?"

"We came across some liquor hid in a hole big enough to stand in. They dug right into the side of the stadium behind the bathrooms," I said.

He looked over at his father.

"That didn't sit too well with him. Or you, I figure," he said.

139

"It didn't, but nothing we did measured up to this. I'll reckon with those bastards after I explain where I've been and get squared away down at the mill."

He suddenly looked away from his father and up at me.

"I think it's past explaining down there, Henry," he said.

He then got up and turned to leave.

Just as he was drawing back the curtain and about to step out, he turned and said, "My mom will be down here in about a half hour. I think you ought to clear out by then, Henry. This has her all tore up. I don't know what she'll say. I appreciate you trying to help him. If I'd have been there and we'd have been three, somebody else'd be in this bed."

With that he was gone. I sat down in a little chair to the side of the bed and looked over at Mr. Spector.

Back in the fight you got pretty good at looking a fellow over and figuring out if he was going to make it. The ones that weren't were a little gray and their eyes were real distant if they was awake. Their cheeks got deep like they'd been dug out some and their breathing got all scratchy.

Mr. Spector was gray near the sides of his neck. You had to look to see it, but I once saw the same on a colored fellow from the 92nd tangled up in the barbed wire, with him still breathing, and he was almost gone when I came upon him. Mr. Spector was a thin man, but his cheeks had nothing to them at all now, and they looked all stoved in. His breathing was not strong.

He was going to die, I knew. Reginald did not. I felt a hole tore through me and I pressed my head down on the side of the bed. I have done so much to push away the killing and dying and it follows me still, every step.

It started getting real hot. I stood up and was suddenly all shaky behind the neck. Here was the shaking back again, and yet I am away from the fields and ruins. I could barely talk.

"Alright, Mr. Spector then. I'll take care of Venable. You pull through here."

It was a senseless thing to say, and I got out of there.

CHAPTER 19

There was no getting past Porter, not on a Monday afternoon when the place was empty and with my hand as it was and a patched up nose. I needed to get it done with.

I came in through the front door. Porter was standing up behind the counter and reading the paper.

"Morning, Porter," I said

He looked at me, staring at the hand.

"That was some scrape you were in up there, Henry."

"Up where, Porter?"

He didn't say anything and held up the paper. He folded it back and handed it to me.

"The whole city knows where, Henry."

It wasn't the main headlines he pointed to, but down in the lower corner of the front page was a little headline that read: *Three Injured, Two Serious, in Stadium Fracas*

It then went on to name "Henry Dawson, war veteran" and "Harold Spector, Negro," but only mentioned the thug in the hospital as a third man.

No mention of the other four that had at us. The story said me and Mr. Spector were stadium workers.

Porter just looked at me. I didn't know what to say, and with my hand and cuts, there was not much to cover that wasn't being said already.

"Henry, you lost sight of things. I'm sorry to see that."

He then handed me a little envelope. It had typed on it one word, "Dawson."

I turned and walked up the stairs. It was only mid-afternoon now, but it being gray, the room was gloomy when I walked in. Sometimes the smoke settled down on the Point and would not quit.

I dropped the envelope on the bed and looked around. I had a window that was pointed up towards the city, and there were some lights on I could make out, even at midday. The north side of town was all covered over in a shadow.

I turned the light on, the little lamp that they gave me when I got out of the service. The Salvation Army had greeted us when we arrived back in New York, and they were handing things out to the boys to welcome them home. I was lucky and got a lamp when most of the men were getting candy or cigars.

After maybe a month back in Poughkeepsie, I'd signed back on in the service at Upton for another two years after the war. After being one of the main places for getting the boys over to the fight, there wasn't a lot of use for it. I helped wind it down, which was sad to see, but it was work and part of the reason I got to be handy with the shovel and a little with the hammer. In '21 the army finally auctioned off everything that was left, and my time there was done.

One of the western boys from the 308th, Carl Lindley, stayed on at Upton until the end. He said he wasn't heading back out west, that farming wasn't what he was meant for after all this, and he was heading down to Baltimore. He said he knew of a big shipyard down here and was going to take the train to Philadelphia, spend a few days with some relatives, and then come on down. He asked me why didn't I join him.

Well, we both made it to Philadelphia alright, but I was eager to get south and not burn up what little money I had before I even got here, so we parted ways, and I told him I'd get things established down here if I could.

As maybe you can guess at this point, Carl did not leave Philly, and I set up shop here alone. The nicest outfit I owned then, and still is, was my army uniform, so I wore it when inquiring down here, and although working on the belt isn't the best job in the world, I got it straightaway, which was a thankful thing because I had not finished up high school back at home.

The first time Porter ever saw me was in my doughboy uniform as I come in through that front door. He saluted me.

"At ease, Private...Dawson," he said with a laugh. He then gave me enough advice to fill a book—on working here and what you do and don't do—and as much as a fellow don't like hearing advice, I was glad for it at the time.

Three years later, and there was this envelope from Beth Steel on my bed with my name on it.

I picked it up and held it over the lamp to see the insides, and sure enough, it was not an empty envelope with this all being a big mistake. I opened it slowly, and my hands were getting a little shaky. It was a yellow sheet folded in three parts.

November 20, 1924

Mr. Dawson:

In light of recent events your employment with Bethlehem Steel has been terminated.

You have two days to vacate the premises. Your final check will be mailed to the address which you may provide to the house superintendent, James Fleming.

Bethlehem Steel

Chapter 20

It was Wednesday now, and I was getting ready to walk downstairs. Everything I owned was boxed up and on the front porch of the house. I hired a cab earlier that morning to come down for me and my belongings at 11:00. If you've never made a call to be picked up from a place you're being turned out of, you are now one better than me. I was through at the stadium, too. The city sent a telegram to me at the hospital, so eager to fire me that they could not wait for the regular mail. All this and Mr. Spector slipping away weighed hard on me, harder than you can picture.

It was awful quiet late morning. You could hear my steps echoing down the wooden staircase like they was marble—it was that still. Porter was there behind the front desk. I don't think he has ever not been there.

"What will you do now, Henry?" he asked.

"I don't know. I'm through at the stadium, too."

"You were set here. Venable was a mistake," he added.

I had no smart comeback like usual this time. He went silent for the first time since I'd known him. He reached across and picked up the envelope with a key that I'd laid on the front desk and put it in my mail slot behind him. It said "H. Dawson – 215," but now had a line through it.

"I've got one more envelope, Porter. It's for Mrs. Foss down at the bank," I said, and pushed it towards him across the counter.

"You should take it down yourself."

I didn't say anything. There was nothing to say.

"Good luck, then," Porter said.

I nodded and turned towards the front of the house. I walked out the door just in time to hear the cab come sputtering down the road and lay on its horn. Before I got in, I took a last look back at the house.

"The bank," I said, and the cabbie knew it and headed towards D Street. I went into the lobby, half hoping to see Mrs. Foss and half hoping to miss her. How could I face her now?

She was not there, so I went up to another gal's spot and filled out a slip to get out my full savings. She took the note and said nothing. I was all banged up, and she was not smiling. I got my money.

"I've got a note for Mrs. Foss, if you can pass it along."

She took it from me under the cage but still said nothing. That was as good as I would do, I could tell, and I went back out the bank's front door.

* * *

I paid a man wearing a greasy cap and coat, and he locked my belongings into a little rundown garage in Fells Point. The roof sagged and the front door looked like it was giving out from the weight of the place pushing down on it. One side had green stuff growing on it, what it was I do not know. The dirtiest alley cat I have ever seen was along the side of the garage trying to get in at something inside a crack in the foundation.

"I've got the key," the man told me. "I live on the second floor right in the alley there to your right. Stairs come up the outside like you can see. You need to get to your things, you come up and knock. I will come down until seven in the evening, and after that it will just have to wait until the next day."

I didn't have much, a copy of *Huckleberry Finn*, an old wooden chair, the lamp, my clothes, and some papers. Beth Steel had provided all the rest. Everything I owned didn't account for much.

With my stuff stowed away, I walked around Fells Point looking for a hotel room I might rent for the month. The money from working at Venable was what kept me out of the poor house. I had at least a few months between me and the street.

After looking at a couple places that didn't seem fit for people to live in, I settled in on the Wharf Hotel. It got its name from Brown's Wharf across the street, which wasn't the newest place—half of it was all rotted away and falling into the Patapsco. It still had a steady flow of ships coming in and out, from what I could see.

This was a sailors' hotel, and although in the army we got pretty filthy because we had no choice, I tend to think we are a cleaner group on the whole.

I took one room with a bed and a rusty sink. There was a bathroom down the hall, and in a way it was like my room at Sparrows Point, but everything was in worse shape. There was a window that pointed out towards the water, and I will say now that the water down at the Point may not have been so dirty compared to what I was smelling here.

I had a small closet and little black painted table that wobbled when the steamers blew their horns. It had a Gideon's Bible on it. I had my uniform with me, hoping it would help me get a place, and I hung it up in the closet before having a seat on the bed. I stared at the scraped up floorboards for a spell and then laid back and closed my eyes.

CHAPTER 21

❧⚜❧

The day of the big game finally came. These were the times after the war when a soldier still was held in high regard, and people didn't much trouble you if you were wearing the army uniform. Some of the boys at the stadium knew me of course, but I was harder to make out in my overcoat, hat, boots, and spats. A police officer came up to me as I walked through the front gate. All banged up and in uniform he might have guessed who I was from the papers. He did a funny thing next, looking at me and then looking at the ground like he'd lost something. He turned up again and was all red. He shuffled his feet and then waved me in with his hand, without a word.

There was a loudspeaker, and I heard the score: Navy leading 12-7, second quarter. I walked over to where Overman told us to gather before heading out to the field. There was Duncan, pacing, and next to him was Carr. Carr was seated on the bench and was staring out towards the field.

I timed it out okay. They were close to the entrance to the field, and I heard the halftime gun sound, and all of a sudden the Navy and Army players alike were running off the field towards them, and Duncan began scrambling around half-crouched like he was ducking for cover. I could see him start shaking Carr, but Norman didn't budge, and I as I got closer I could hear Duncan yelling, "Here they come, Sergeant."

Carr, sitting still, knew that they wasn't going to run him over. He didn't move and lit a cigarette.

"Sit down, Duncan. They're just passing through here to the locker room," I heard him shout out of the side of his mouth above the noise.

Duncan took a seat next to Carr, and only the players now were between me and the boys. About halfway into the tunnel, the players broke off to their side of the entrance and headed into the locker rooms.

With all the clatter it was a good time to join the boys without being noticed. I worked through the last few stragglers and a couple of Army players smiled when they passed and one even saluted me although I was just a private and now not even that.

Finally all the cleats and shoulder pads and players were through, and I was able to talk.

"Henry!" Duncan said, before I got a word out. He shook my hand with both of his and squeezed real hard.

Carr didn't get up and only looked up at me. My being there now was trouble and he wasn't getting too close.

"Duncan, Carr," I said, patting Carr on the knee to bother him, and took a seat on the bench. He saw my bad hand poked out from under my uniform but didn't say anything, my face was bad enough. We sat there and heard out on the field the announcer clearing his throat.

"Ladies and gentlemen, we are honored to have here today two veterans of the Great War," the announcer said as the Army band marched to the center of the field with the cadets right behind them, divided into their units.

I started gripping the bench and rocking a little bit, I don't know why, and Carr saw me and got up and moved away quickly. Duncan was looking at me rocking. The announcer was going on about the 308th and how terrific we'd all been, like he was reviewing a play.

"Henry?" Duncan asked, real worried.

I turned, looked at him, and stopped my rocking, seeing how uneasy he was getting. Duncan never came out of the woods, not all of him. I can't help wonder the same about myself, seeing him like this and feeling how I do. I stood up and grabbed him by the arm.

"Come on, Duncan. We're ready."

I smiled the biggest smile I could manage then I started walking slowly towards the field, with Carr and Duncan falling in behind me. Soon we were on the grassy area just outside the cinder track. Overman stepped out from our left and walked in front of the three of us, blocking our path. I knew he would be there, but I'd still held out hope that he might not.

"Step back, Dawson. You're no longer part of this," he said.

But I was, as was Mr. Spector, now dying in his bed. We were more part of this place than Overman would ever be.

I stared at him. He was not going to try to wrestle a soldier back away from the track. Not with the mayor here. Not with the President here. We were in plain sight, where men like Overman and Russell did not do so well.

I felt his arm grab mine, but it had not fight in it and after a moment he let loose and backed away from the three of us. The band struck up a song and damn if they weren't playing a march song from Camp Upton. As it carried to us and echoed off the walls throughout Venable, I could hear Duncan begin singing the words, real quietly, but as certain to him as they were to us.

The long line we march ever onward
We trust it fore and aft,
We push through darkness at our shoulder
And together through we pass.

The band paused between verses and suddenly Duncan's hand clung to my arm from behind, and I could feel it shaking.

"Move in, Carr, three astride, our overcoats touching," I yelled to Carr.

He stopped and stared at me.

"Goddamn it, Carr, Duncan is not moving unless we go astride. Let's go!"

He shot forward and took his place to my left, with Duncan to the right. The music struck up again and we were all astride, like we were in the parades in New York before we shipped out. We did not hear the mortar fire or sickly whistles or horrible cries that were calling our names from afar. We just heard the crowds on Broadway, and music. Duncan's hand stayed gripping my arm down by the wrist and the three of us marched so tightly our shoulders practically touched.

As we pushed out onto the cinder track, the crowd shot up to its feet before us and roared, and they were around us to every side, like a forest. Their roar was so strong it filled your chest as if their voices were your own. Duncan's grip let go and his arm fell away. As we strode along the track and moved towards the President's box I could see him to my right out of the corner of my eye, moving steadfast again. There was no hesitation, no worry that each step led further into something horrible. In the sunlight he looked to me like the boy I knew from the farmhouse, long ago. The boy who could sleep like a baby.

For a moment, all was not lost.

Epilogue

On November 29, 1924 Army defeated Navy 12-0
before 80,000 fans at Venable, increasingly referred
to in print by then simply as "the Stadium." In
attendance were a host of dignitaries including the
mayor, the governor, and President Coolidge and
his wife. The game was broadcast by seven radio
stations, a remarkable total for the time. Famed
sportswriter Grantland Rice called it "probably the
greatest gathering that ever saw a football battle in
the East."

The stadium's structural problems persisted
throughout its quarter century of life. By 1933, the
year Prohibition ended, the stadium was running
consistently in the red. Showing the same resolve
from whence it was built, it persisted long enough
to help establish Baltimore as a city of major league
stature, much as its original designers had hoped.
The stadium was gradually razed in the late 1940s
and replaced in the same location by its successor,
Memorial Stadium. The only visible reminders of
its existence are a pair of iron torchieres that once
adorned the upper corners of its grand façade. They

now spend their days guarding a modest front yard just blocks away from their original home.

Sparrows Point continued to expand from the 1920s, reaching its greatest production in the mid-1950s. Its prosperity proved the ruin of the company town, as ever larger sections of its neighborhoods were demolished to make room for the expanding mill operations. By the mid-1970s, the town was completely consumed by mill expansions.

The site of Bay Shore Park now hosts a state park, and Mrs. Foss's sunken wooden steamers still silently dot the banks of Curtis Creek.

ABOUT THE AUTHOR

❧

Tom Flynn is a freelance writer and has contributed to the *Washington Post*, the *Baltimore Sun*, the *Wall Street Journal*, *PressBox*, and *Maryland Life*. His first book, *Baseball in Baltimore*, was published in 2008. Links to Tom's articles can be found at fieldmagazine. blogspot.com.

Breinigsville, PA USA
30 January 2011
254424BV00001B/11/P